MYSTERY IN STUDIO 13

DOROTHY WOOLFOLK

SCHOLASTIC INC.
New York Toronto London Auckland Sydney Tokyo

For Candy Lampasi, muy simpatico

Cover photograph by Owen Brown

ISBN 0-590-32865-4

12 11 10 9 8 7 6 5 4 3 2 1 2 4 5 6 7 8/8

Printed in the U.S.A. 06

MYSTERY IN STUDIO 13

A DONNA ROCKFORD MYSTERY

DONNA ROCKFORD MYSTERIES

Mother, Where Are You?

Who Killed Daddy?

Death of a Dancer

Murder in Washington/Body on the Beach

Abbey Is Missing

Mystery in Studio 13

"F*ifteen minutes to show time . . . fifteen minutes!*"

The voice crackled over the TV studio loudspeakers and filled the studio audience with excitement.

"I can't believe we're really here," Abbey Rockford said breathlessly, looking around the audience. "Pete, you're such a genius for getting these tickets. And front row seats!"

"Don't thank me," Pete O'Brien said. "Thank my cousin Barbara. She works for the show, and she's got a small bit part today. She wangled the tickets so she'd have some fans in the audience."

They were seated in the front row of a television studio at WGBL-TV in Philadelphia. There were a hundred plush red theater seats in the room, although it looked like a larger auditorium on television. Just about every seat was filled with a teenager, except for the one between Abbey and Pete O'Brien, her sister's boyfriend.

In front of them was the raised stage for "The Teenage Talent Show." That area was intensely lit by black-sheathed spotlights shining down from heavy iron bars across the ceiling. Between the stage set and the audience was a row of cameras and other equipment, as well as cameramen and technicians doing their various jobs — from stacking cue cards to checking props.

Abbey Rockford, enchanted by the growing excitement in the studio, tugged at Pete's sleeve.

"Oh, Pete, we'll cheer our heads off for Barbara," Abbey promised. "Won't we, Jane?"

"You bet." Jane Morrison, Abbey's best friend, grinned. "Wait till the kids at school find out that we actually got to watch a taping of 'The Teenage Talent Show.' They'll die of jealousy."

"Maybe we'll show up on camera!" Abbey tossed her long black hair from her face. "Do I look all right?"

"You're a knockout," Pete said. "And so's Donna. But where is she? I can't figure it. She's always on time."

"She'd better get here soon," Jane said. "The ticket says, 'Doors close at five-thirty.' "

"She's in the school library, writing a

paper on the criminal mind for Professor Gordon," Abbey said. "Honestly, she's obsessed by that subject. I'll bet she completely forgot the time." Though she sounded annoyed, Abbey was privately pleased that her sister, Donna Rockford, a sophomore at the University of Pennsylvania, was also gaining recognition as a talented amateur detective.

"Abbey! Look!" Jane said. "That's Monte Clark! The announcer!" She pointed to a tall, silver-haired man of about forty who had just walked onto the stage. "Isn't he gorgeous?"

"I don't know. He looks — different in person." Abbey was disappointed. "Thinner — and older, too."

"And look at the set! It's so tiny," Jane said. "Isn't it amazing how big it looks on the TV screen?"

"Ten minutes to go . . . ten minutes. . . ."

"Good evening, friends, and welcome to the eighty-fifth edition of 'The Teenage Talent Show.'" The tall, genial announcer of WGBL-TV's hit show beamed at the audience — a lively crowd of squealing, screaming teenagers, mixed with a sprinkling of older people, mostly parents.

"We have a great show lined up for you tonight," Monte Clark continued. "I know you're going to have a wonderful time."

"Maybe we will, if Donna ever gets here," Pete said, looking toward the rear of the auditorium.

"Sshhh, Pete," Abbey said impatiently. "I want to hear this." She indicated a little tableau that was taking place onstage.

Monte Clark had stepped back a few feet to look at his script, and a man with a clipboard hurried over to him. From their front row seats, Abbey could overhear snatches of frantic, whispered conversation onstage.

"We have only three cameras. . . . Can't stand over them with a whip, . . ." the man said.

"You're the director — but *he* pays the salaries," Monte said. "Don't ever forget that."

"What about the union, Monte? They'll never stand for it. . . ."

"Wait'll Rick hears. He'll flip out. . . . Not enough close-ups. . . . You know his temper, . . ." Monte Clark said worriedly.

"Abbey, they're not talking about Rick Roberts, are they?" Jane whispered.

"Absolutely not," Abbey said. "*My* Rick Roberts? He's an angel."

"Where is the angel?" Pete asked. "I can't wait to see Mr. Perfect in person."

"Don't be jealous, Pete." Abbey patted his hand. "You've got your good points. It's just that Rick is something else."

At that moment Abbey felt a tap on her shoulder and looked up to see her sister standing there, panting for breath, her smooth brown hair windblown, her hazel eyes glowing.

"Donna! Where've you been?" Abbey said.

"Running all the way," Donna said, flinging her white wool scarf back and zipping open her bright blue jacket. "Whew! I got all involved at the library." She turned and beamed at Pete and Jane. "Hi, people. Excuse me for being so late, but I got all tied up with my paper."

As Abbey flashed an I-told-you-so look at Pete, Donna continued, "The more I study, the more I realize how terrifically complex the criminal mind is. Fascinating."

Abbey patted the seat beside her. "Sit down, brain. The show's about to start and I'm so excited I can't stand it!"

"Five minutes to go, everybody . . . five minutes."

Monte Clark stepped to the front of the stage apron once more and said, "In just a few minutes, you're going to meet Rick Roberts — in person. I want to know how you're going to welcome him. Let's hear it, folks."

There was a huge burst of applause and screaming.

It had taken only one year for Rick Roberts, the host of "The Teenage Talent Show," to become the hottest star on TV. The secret lay in his image. More than half the audience was wearing "Teenage Talent" T-shirts. For once, their parents approved of a teenager's idol. Rick was so clean-cut, and all-American — the eternally boyish type — that everyone from six to sixty loved him. Handsome, strait-laced, athletic — he was as much admired by their parents as by the teenagers his show was aimed at.

"Oh, Donna," Abbey said. "I can't bear it." She looked at Donna's outfit — a striped blue-and-white cotton shirt, with a thin purple string tie at the collar. "Listen, I've got an extra Rick T-shirt." She dug into her tote bag and pulled out one identical to her own. "Here, put it on!"

Donna smiled and said, "Thanks, Abbey, but I don't really want to. That's for his real fans — like you and Jane. I don't think I've even watched his show more than twice. He's talented. . . ."

"Talented? He's just the host of the show," Pete protested. "He doesn't do any entertaining. It's all done by the contestants — teenage singers and dancers and comics. What's all the fuss?"

"Pete, you kill me!" Abbey rolled her eyes as Jane groaned in sympathy. "First of all, Rick does entertain! He opens every show with a fantastic stunt. Either it's a magic trick, or a gymnastic stunt, or a comedy routine. . . ."

"Four minutes to go . . . four minutes."

As the offstage speaker quieted, heads started to turn in the audience. From the rear of the auditorium, a stunning blond woman in a white leather jumpsuit was moving swiftly down the right aisle, with a uniformed usher escorting her. In dead silence, everyone watched her move sensuously behind the usher. The effect of her platinum blond hair, white leather suit, and slightly overripe figure — slim waist and richly curved bosom and hips — was dazzling.

"That's Lana Lawrence," Abbey whispered. "She used to be Rick's girl friend. But they broke up."

"I remember now," Donna said. "Wasn't there some kind of scandal?"

"Right!" Jane said. "No one knows why they split. They were such a glamorous couple. She was on the way to being a big star in Hollywood."

"But after Rick stopped seeing her, she dropped out of sight," Abbey said. "No one knows where she went."

"Some people said she had a nervous breakdown," Jane contributed.

"Who knows?" Abbey said. "The studio ripped up her contract, and she was through as a film star."

"Where did you read all that trash?" Pete asked. "In those junk tabloid newspapers?"

Abbey ignored Pete's remark. "Doesn't she look terrific, Jane?"

"Yes," Jane said enthusiastically. "I'm glad. Poor thing. It must be awful trying to live without the divine Rick Roberts, once you've known him."

"Since you both seem to have the inside track," Pete said, "why did Rick and Lana break up? I won't sleep tonight unless I find out."

"Your jealousy is showing, Pete," Abbey said loftily. "Cut the sarcasm. Jane and I are here to see a truly wonderful person. Oh, why bother? You'll see for yourself in a few minutes!"

Backstage, the divine Rick Roberts' face was crimson with anger.

"My script! My cues! Doesn't anyone in this stupid excuse for a production team know where anything is?"

Rick was standing amid thick cables, rushing stagehands, and other frantic technicians. He had surfer blond hair and piercing blue eyes; a long white terrycloth robe showed off his golden tan. At the moment his hands were on his hips and his foot was tapping impatiently.

"Where's Bonnie? That little idiot! She was supposed to give me my script changes at four o'clock. Now I have to go out there in two minutes and be brilliant and charming for those pimply faced teenagers." He stopped for breath. "I need my script! *Abe!*" He roared the name.

Abe Hazelkorn, producer of "The Teenage Talent Show," came running.

"Not to worry, Rick. I've got the changes right here." Abe handed him a sheaf of papers. "You know I'm looking after you, Rick baby. The copy machine broke down and Bonnie had to go down the street to get these made."

"Oh, sure, the old copy machine alibi. Everybody's got an excuse. Even the stupid script girl." Rick flung the pages down on his desk. "But what can you expect, with a father like hers?"

Instantly Abe gestured toward the ceiling, where a gray-haired man was securing a set of parallel bars to a rigging suspended from the rafters.

"Rick, please," Abe said quietly. "He can hear you."

"So what? You're missing the point," Rick said coldly. "I *told* you to get rid of him, Abe. He's the oldest living incompetent stagehand in TV." He broke off as a pretty young woman of about 19 or 20, with honey-colored hair, came hurrying over.

"Bonnie! I've been waiting for you! You're late!" Rick tightened the belt of his robe with a vicious twist. "No more excuses like the copying machine. Got it?"

"Yes, Mr. Roberts." She looked timorously at him, then up at the eaves where her father was, then back at the glowering star. "It won't happen again," she said, turning to leave.

"Wait up! I'm not finished with you yet!" As the girl froze in front of him, Rick thumbed through the pages of script before him. "I want to check this garbage out!"

"So now he's a star," a nearby cameraman whispered to his colleague. "That entitles him to act like a high-class creep."

"So what else is new?" the second cameraman said. He was an old-timer in TV and had seen it all before.

"If only those crazy kids out there could

see their hero," the first cameraman said. "They've got clout, those teenagers. They could bad-mouth him, and, in no time, he'd be out of the business."

"*Out!*" Rick Roberts said. "I want Howard Reilly out! Isn't that what I told you, Abe?"

"Rick," Abe Hazelkorn said, "have a heart. Howard's been with this studio for over twenty years. . . ."

"Don't give me that sob story about how great he used to be." Rick flung a pencil down. "I can't get this show on week after week with memories — I need top people."

"The union won't allow it . . ." Abe protested.

"I don't care about the union. I'll dream up a story you can hand them." Rick was getting angrier.

"But you can't do that. . . ."

"But me no buts. He *goes.*" Rick pushed his desk microphone to one side, opened the script book in front of him again, and glanced at the copy for the show's opening. As he did, he saw a slim, mild-looking man heading toward the pit, where the musicians were tuning up. It was Rex Vicente, the show's orchestra leader.

"Hey, Wreck!" he yelled. "Wait up!"

The orchestra leader stopped short. "You want me, Rick?"

"Who else? I said 'Wreck,' didn't I?" Rick Roberts jeered. "Your band fell apart during dress rehearsal. I've heard livelier music played at a funeral in Nowhere, North

Carolina." He aimed a menacing finger at the bandleader. "Jolt some life into them, understand?"

"Right, Rick." Rex Vicente unglued himself from where he stood and, tight-lipped, walked down to the pit. He seemed to be in perfect control, but the score sheets in his hand were visibly shaking.

"Two minutes to show time . . . two minutes."

"Isn't Rick great?" Abbey said as she and Jane watched Rex Vicente mount the podium, then turn and wave at the audience, who greeted him with a roar. "Look at the people who work for him! Rex Vicente is so good, the Lincoln Symphony Orchestra offered him a job last month."

"Rick nicknamed Rex 'The Wreck.' It's a running gag on the show," Jane volunteered. She bit into a chocolate bar and offered it to Pete, who shook his head *no*. "Rick is an absolute dream! I adore him!"

High up in the eaves on a platform, Howard Reilly took a deep breath. His face was pasty gray.

"I can take the abuse," he said to a prop man nearby. "Honestly I can, for myself. But when he rips me up in front of my daughter, I could . . ."

"Forget it, Howard," the man said. "You've lasted longer on this show than anyone else. . . ."

"If he lets me go now, it's the end of my pension plan," Howard Reilly said. "I mean, I'll lose the big benefits. And he knows it. I've only got three more months to go."

"Ssh," his helper warned. "Something's going on down there. What is it?"

Onstage, Rick Roberts was glancing through the partially opened black velvet curtain. He jumped up from his desk and said, "I don't believe this! What's *she* doing out there?" His eyes stared unbelievingly at the glamorous blonde in the third row right of center.

He spun around and started to shout. "All right! Why didn't somebody tell me Lana Lawrence is here?" Then he broke off as a blond young man, slim and pale, wearing thick horn-rimmed eyeglasses, stopped before him.

"Johnny Argyle! What are you doing here?" Rick said suspiciously. "I thought you were starting your vacation today."

"Yes, Mr. Roberts, I am," the young man said timidly. "I just wanted to make sure everything was right for the opening stunt."

"Well, as it so happens, there is something you can do, Johnny." Rick paused, then shook a finger at him. "But if you think you're getting paid overtime for showing up today, you've got another think coming."

"Oh, no, Mr. Roberts. I wouldn't think of it," Johnny said quickly. "What do you want me to do?"

Johnny Argyle carried the impressive title

— with an unimpressive salary — of production assistant. When the cast needed a dozen Danish and coffee for the ten o'clock break, they sent Johnny. When pencils had to be sharpened, or someone was needed to sort the mail, Johnny did it. As on every TV show, there was always a need for a gofer. Johnny was the show's gofer: "Johnny, go for this; Johnny, go for that."

Right now Johnny was watching intently as Rick grabbed a piece of paper, wrote down instructions, and handed it to Johnny.

"Be sure to take care of this right away," the star snapped. "And get that right up to Reilly!"

The young gofer glanced at the sheet. "But there isn't time for this, Mr. Roberts! You can't expect the prop man to . . ." He stopped short as Rick Roberts snatched the paper from his hand.

"Here, I'll take it to him myself!" The star glared at the young boy and angrily walked away.

Johnny Argyle watched him go, then crossed over to stage left and bent over something blue on the floor. It was a cross made of adhesive tape. Johnny stared again at the floor, hesitated, drew a determined breath, and bent down to the blue tape cross once more.

As Rick Roberts walked to center stage, waving to the audience, there was a near riot.

"*Rick-ie . . . Rick-ie. . . .*" The famous chant

that greeted his entrance to every show started up and swelled until it filled the hall, only fading away as Rick Roberts modestly held up his hand to quiet them.

"Are we going to have fun tonight?" he asked.

The roars and squeals gave him the answer he wanted. He looked around the audience searchingly, left and right, then did a carefully planned double take as he saw Lana Lawrence, sitting in the third row on the aisle. He blew her a kiss, waved once more to the audience, and spoke to them.

"Thank you for that wonderful welcome," he said. "You know what makes 'The Teenage Talent Show' such a success? Not the performers. Not me. *You.* You, my wonderful fans. Give yourselves a big hand."

"How about a hand for the orchestra, led by our own Rex the Wreck — Rex Vicente." Another round of applause and raucous cries followed. When the noise stopped, Rick said, "He's the only bandleader in America who thinks Beethoven's Fifth is a bottle of whiskey," and walked off to the laughter of the audience.

The APPLAUSE sign lighted up, blinking furiously, and the audience clapped wildly. Rex Vicente raised his baton, the sign flashed ON THE AIR, and the band broke into the show's theme song.

In the wings, a hairdresser ran a comb through Rick's hair while a makeup girl gave his face a final powdering. Rick pushed them away and then, smiling, walked confidently onstage to the podium from which he hosted the show.

A thunderous roar greeted him as the excitement in the studio reached its highest pitch. The star waited for the uproar to die down, then looked into the camera, smiled, and started to speak. "Good evening, fans and friends all over America." He smiled again, white teeth flashing in his sunburned face. As he tossed his yellow mane of hair back impatiently, the home audience across the nation could now hear the studio audience cheering.

"We have a great show for you tonight, I promise you. You're going to love it. Some of the most talented teenagers in America will be performing, trying to win the big prize." Rick Roberts stepped down from the podium and opened his white-and-gold robe. "But first — my own performance."

He took off his robe, revealing an electric blue gym suit.

"Here it comes," Abbey whispered to Pete. "His opening stunt. Now you'll see how talented he is!"

Onstage Rick was saying, ". . . want to encourage all of you here in the studio and out there in this great country of ours to keep fit." He crossed over to right center stage. "Just to show you how easy it is to do gymnastics. . . ." He broke off and looked down at the orchestra leader in the pit. "If I can have a drum roll . . . yes, I'm speaking to you, Wreck. . . ."

As the drummer beat a tattoo on his bass drum, Rick Roberts grinned and looked up toward the eaves. He made a face, then said, "Okay, lower away, old man." He smiled, waved his hand upward in a friendly gesture to the unseen stagehand, and turned back to the audience.

"Here it comes!" he said. From above could be heard the cranking of equipment being slowly lowered toward the stage.

"And here goes nothing!" Keeping his eyes on the camera, the star smiled and flashed the mischievous look his fans loved. So intent was he that he did not see the equipment over his head take a sudden, sharp drop. Down it plunged, faster and faster. It took only a split second and then it was too late.

The heavy wood and metal set of parallel bars thudded against him and hurled him to the floor.

In one split second, it was all over for Rick Roberts.

TWO

Studio 13 instantly became a frozen house of horror. The icy chill of disaster emanated from the stage, gripping the crew, the audience, the stagehands up in the rafters — everyone. Amid shrieks and moans from the onlookers, Abe Hazelkorn, the producer, came running out of the control booth.

As the show's staff milled around the body of Rick Roberts onstage, the television monitors flashed the words PLEASE STAND BY, replacing onscreen the gruesome scene for the national TV audience.

"Poor guy! He didn't stand a chance!" Pete's voice cracked. He turned to Donna. "Are you okay?"

"Okay . . . I'm okay, Pete," Donna repeated almost mindlessly. She was stunned by the tragedy. How could such a thing have happened? TV people were highly skilled, dedicated technicians. They had to be — especially on national network shows, where they were seen regularly by millions of people.

Donna surveyed the chaos onstage, then carefully scanned each face of all those who were connected with "The Teenage Talent Show." They were now massed together around the fallen star, even as the huge velvet curtain hastily drew to a close in the center, shutting off the view from the shocked audience. Donna looked quickly about the small auditorium, where ushers and staff were trying to offer comfort as best they could to the audience.

Something made her turn and look across the crowd toward where Lana Lawrence had sat, toward where Rick Roberts, poor Rick, had blown a last kiss. The seat was empty. That was strange, Donna thought. Where was the actress?

In the next instant, Donna turned to her sister and Jane. Incredibly, sirens wailed to a stop outside the theater, and both police and ambulance medics came pounding down the aisle and disappeared through a doorway leading to the stage. As Abbey's dark eyes followed their progress, Donna saw the tears cascade down her sister's face. Once before

Abbey had witnessed a similar disaster — the awful night when famed Russian dancer Boris Dukov had died onstage during *Swan Lake*. The shock now was just as intense, just as ineradicable as it was then. Donna threw her arms around Jane first and spoke softly to her, while she indicated with her eyes that Pete should go over and comfort Abbey, although it was plain to see that Pete was as upset as anyone there. Boys were weeping along with girls, the young with the old, but some were restraining themselves enough to offer help to those who needed it more.

"Pete, can you run Abbey and Jane back to the house?" Donna asked.

"Sure thing," Pete said. "They don't belong here."

For once, Abbey offered no resistance, just waited mutely to follow Donna and Pete's lead.

"If my mother isn't home," Donna said in an aside to Pete, "please call my dad. Jane and Abbey shouldn't be alone."

"Don't worry, Donna. I'll stick with them until someone gets there," Pete said.

Donna kissed Abbey and Jane and told them, "I'm very proud of you both. It's a horrible, awful thing to have happened, but you're both standing up to it much better than a lot of the grown-ups here." She patted them lovingly. "You and Jane go home, Abbey, and I'll stick around here a bit and try to do my thing. Maybe I can find out how and why this terrible accident happened." She paused. "I don't understand it at all."

Upset though Abbey was, the look of concentration on her sister's face helped to somehow lessen the pain. Abbey extravagantly admired Donna's cool, clear logic, her dispassionate view of events as they happened, her extraordinary ability to focus on the overall picture.

What is Donna thinking? Abbey wondered. Was it possible — the thought was too awful — that it hadn't been an accident that killed Rick Roberts?

"It's impossible," Abbey said, walking out with Pete, Donna, and Jane to the rear of the theater. "Of course it was an accident. Wasn't it, Donna?"

"That's what everyone's going to try to find out, Abbey." She kissed her sister and Jane again. "You go ahead. I'll get back to the house sooner than soon."

As the two girls left with Pete, Donna hurried down the aisle toward the stage, where she turned left and went through the door that led backstage.

The scene was unreal. Donna saw uniformed policemen milling about onstage, as the last of the ambulance people left by a rear exit. The only evidence of Rick Roberts' tragedy was a simple green cloth covering the portion of the stage where it had happened.

As Donna took a couple of tentative steps forward, a blue-clad policeman stepped in front of her, barring her way.

"You can't come in here, girlie," he said. "You'll be in the way."

"Excuse me, officer," Donna started to explain, but the policeman stopped her.

"There's been a terrible accident here, kiddo," he said with a condescending nod. "We've got to clear this area. No teenage fanatics needed here." He jerked a hand toward the exit. "Get going." As she hesitated, he said, "*Now.*" Donna looked around, hoping to see someone in the crowd of people who could help her. *If only Mario Garcia were here*, she was thinking.

The policeman, getting nasty, said, "How many times do you have to be told?" his tone crackling with irritation, when suddenly the police captain spoke up in a loud, authoritative voice.

"Hey, Hennessey! Let that young lady alone. Do you hear me?"

Donna took a closer look at the official elbowing his way through the crowd toward them. Just as she recognized Captain John Gavin, he made it to her side.

"Donna Rockford — it's a pleasure to see you, young woman." The captain looked at the patrolman. "This is Donna Rockford, Hennessey. The name mean anything to you?"

The young cop, trapped, fumbled for a way to respond. "Well, sure. I mean, I don't exactly know her. . . ."

"She's a friend of Detective Garcia's and" — the police captain smiled approvingly at her — "she's given us a hand before. She stays, Hennessey." He said to Donna, "I'm sorry, Donna."

"Excuse me, miss," the young patrolman said. "I didn't know. . . ."

"It's okay. You were doing your job." Donna smiled at him, but privately thought he didn't have to be so abrupt; he hadn't given her a chance to say anything.

"Can you fill us in?" Captain Gavin said. "I assume you were here for the show."

"That's right. My kid sister is — was — a big fan of Rick Roberts," Donna said, swallowing. "Pete O'Brien — you remember him, Captain?" When the captain nodded, Donna continued, "Pete got us tickets and everything was going pretty smoothly, when suddenly . . ." She broke off as a new voice inserted itself into the conversation.

"And what are you doing here? This is a surprise," the voice was saying. Donna turned to see Detective Mario Garcia.

"Mario! Am I glad to see you!" Donna looked affectionately at the tall, handsome, red-haired young detective. Then, remembering that Mario's superior was right there, she added, "I was just giving Captain Gavin a rundown on the accident. I was here when it happened."

"Right," Captain Gavin said. "It doesn't hurt to have that extra little edge when you're getting information from witnesses."

Detective Garcia said, "I just got a seven-oh-six on the car radio, so I hustled right over."

"Glad you did," the police captain said. "This is a nasty one. Chances are it's an accident, but who knows? A big star like Rick Roberts is bound to have enemies."

"That's odd that you should say that, Captain," Donna said. "Our seats were down front, and there certainly seemed to be some kind of squabbling going on backstage."

As she went on to explain, a policeman hurried up. "Captain Gavin! We've got everyone connected with the show lined up over there." He indicated a group of people standing against the rear wall. Among them, Donna recognized Monte Clark, the announcer; Rex Vicente, the bandleader; and the young script girl who had hurried over to Rick just before the show began. She looked for the tall, skinny boy with eyeglasses, who had been fumbling with something on the floor of the stage and calling up to someone above just before the show began. He was nowhere to be seen.

Mario Garcia, his eyes on Donna, said, "What is it? Something bothering you, Donna?"

"Yes. Someone who should be here and isn't," Donna said.

"Who's that?" the captain asked. When Donna explained, he said quickly to the young cop beside him, "Go over there, find out who the kid with eyeglasses was, and tell our men to take a good look for him — pronto!"

Donna felt a slight shock as she realized that unwittingly she had probably established the young man as a suspect. Suspect? But that was only if a crime had been committed. And that brought up again the ugly thought: *Why had that equipment fallen? Was it an accident?*

"I'm going to question those people over there," Captain Gavin said. "Come on, you two." As he started off, Mario Garcia took Donna's elbow, squeezed it, and said, "Hey, what do you know? You're really beginning to rate with my boss." Donna gave a little shiver and Mario saw that she was still very shaken up by the recent events. "Was it that bad, Donna?" he said.

"It was awful, Mario," she said simply. She looked at him with grateful hazel eyes. "I'm so glad you're here."

"Now let me get this straight," Captain Gavin said to the assemblage in the rear of the stage. "You're the producer," this to Abe Hazelkorn; "you're the bandleader," to Rex Vicente; and so he went all down the line, until he got to the young script girl.

"My name is Bonnie Reilly," she said, "and yes, I had some last minute changes for Rick, and . . ."

"Reilly?" the police captain said. "Any relation to the grip up there? Howard Reilly?"

"I'm his daughter," Bonnie Reilly said harshly. "I want to go up and see my dad. Where is he?"

"Just a minute," the captain began.

"If you're looking for the gofer, Johnny Argyle," Abe Hazelkorn volunteered, "Bonnie should know. She's his girl friend."

"Is that so?" Captain Gavin's steel gray eyes surveyed the young script girl.

"Yes," Bonnie Reilly said quickly. "Johnny and I are going steady. He left on vacation, but I don't know where he's going. I didn't even see him today."

"Captain Gavin!" a voice from above yelled. "Come on up and take a look!" Those on-stage looked up to the rafters where an earnest-faced policeman was bending over and motioning wildly. "You've got to see this!"

Captain Gavin said, "Take over, Hennessey. Everyone stays here until they explain what they were doing when the equipment dropped. Got that?"

Patrolman Hennessey took a notebook from his inside jacket. "Got it, Captain."

As Captain Gavin started for the iron stairs leading up to the rafters, he said out of the side of his mouth, "Come on, you two," and Mario Garcia and Donna quickly fell into step behind him.

"Wait!" Bonnie Reilly called after them, then broke away, ignoring the policeman who tried in vain to hold her back.

"If you're looking for my father," she said, distraught, "I was up there and couldn't find him anyplace." She appealed to Mario, who was the last one mounting the stairs. "Please, officer, can't I go with you?"

Mario Garcia looked into her unhappy face, noted her clouded blue eyes, her hair and clothes in disarray, and said, "Come on, kid. We'll all take a look."

At the top of the stairs, Captain Gavin walked along a narrow catwalk toward the policeman who had motioned him to come up.

"How do you like this?" The cop indicated two hooks and an iron pipe attached to a heavy beam. From one hook, a thick strand of raveled rope dangled limply in the air, telling its own mute story. Obviously the parallel bars had been suspended from it. Instead of running through the two heavy iron hooks, somehow it had been attached to only one of the hooks and the weight on the single hook had been too great, ripping it from the mooring above.

Donna and Detective Garcia looked at each other, each knowing the story as clearly as if it had been told to them.

"How could that happen?" Detective Garcia said. "Anyone could tell that equipment needed extra bracing up here."

"What's this?" Donna picked up a clipboard with a sheet of paper on it. At the top was the heading SET FOR EQUIPMENT FOR OPENING GYM STUNT, ROBERTS. Then there was a hasty diagram, but half the sheet was ripped off irregularly.

"Where's that Reilly man?" Captain Gavin asked his subordinate. "Any sign of him?"

"There wasn't a soul here when I came up, Captain," the cop said.

"Did you look in the wings? How about over there?" The captain indicated some draperies covering the rafters at either end.

Donna, meanwhile, started toward a set of four or five steps leading up to an area painted black, as all the walls and ceilings were, but with a dim red light glowing.

Mario, following her, said, "I get it. This must be an exit." He watched as Donna pulled back a black cloth revealing a heavy iron fire exit door, then went to her side as she pushed it open. A gush of cold air rushed in, and they saw beyond the opening a thin, spiderlike fire escape extending into the darkness. They looked down at something that seemed to be blocking their way out. At first glance it was a lumpy dark bundle. But a second look revealed the body of a man lying across the grating. The shock of white hair told them even before they saw his face who it was: the missing stagehand, Howard Reilly.

His face and body showed no sign of life at all.

THREE

"What's going on, anyway?" the white-coated paramedic said as he rushed with his partner out of the General Hospital ambulance toward the stage door of Studio 13. "Two emergencies in twenty minutes!"

His partner, a trim young woman in white, racing up the stairs beside him, said, "The call-in said we might be too late. I hope we're not. Come on!"

When they reached the head of the stairs, the door was flung open by Donna Rockford. "Thank goodness you're here," she said. "That was quick."

"What's it all about, sister?" the male paramedic asked, coming through the doorway.

"Seems like they're dropping like flies in here."

The female paramedic cast him an annoyed look as Donna said, "Follow me and see for yourself!" She headed up the iron fire escape two steps at a time. "This way — it's faster!"

The three sped up to the third landing, where Donna stepped back and the medics took over.

Before them, Howard Reilly lay on his back, his eyes shut, his face ashen and distorted.

A small group circled the stagehand's body. Detective Garcia had his arm around Bonnie Reilly to support her. Suddenly she cried out.

"Save him! Please save him! Don't let my father die!" she begged the white-coated medics.

Sobbing, she dropped to her knees and was about to fling herself on her father's outstretched body, but Mario Garcia grabbed her and pulled her back.

"Just let them do their job, Bonnie," he said. "That's the best way to help."

"I — I just wanted to hold his hand," Bonnie said helplessly.

"Here, let me," Donna said to Mario as she gently took Bonnie aside. The two medics looked up gratefully and bent to the task before them.

The woman medic lifted Reilly's wrist,

then felt the indentation at the base of his throat. "I can't find a pulse. Let's try some oxygen."

The male medic clamped an oxygen mask over Howard Reilly's mouth as his partner tripped the switch on the portable oxygen tank. For long, agonizing minutes the two medics devoted themselves to a valiant attempt to resuscitate the stricken man. There was no visible reaction.

At one point, Donna heard the female medic say quietly to her partner, "We've finally raised a pulse. It looks like a stroke to me. What do you think?"

The male paramedic shrugged his shoulders, as if to disagree, when suddenly there was a slight tremor in Reilly's body.

"Easy does it," the male medic said. "I think he's finally coming around."

"Dad! Dad!" Bonnie Reilly exclaimed. "Oh, thank God!"

The female paramedic looked up and said cautiously, "Let's try to be as calm as possible. You just send good thoughts to him, dear, while we see what we can do to help him."

Bonnie nodded and stared fixedly at her father, while Donna held on to her.

"What about that bruise on the side of his head?" Captain Gavin asked.

"Looks as though it happened when he fell," the male paramedic answered. "Please, Captain, we can't talk now. We're trying to pull him through."

Minutes later, the female paramedic

stood up. "He stands a chance." She went to Bonnie and said, "Your father definitely had a stroke. We won't know until we get him to the hospital whether it happened because of the blow to his head or if that came afterward when he fell." She touched Bonnie gently on the cheek. "You can ride with us in the ambulance; he's unconscious, but I think you should be near him, to comfort him."

At the young woman's words, Bonnie straightened her shoulders and seemed to regain better control of herself. She whispered, "Thank you, doctor," and followed as her father was carried carefully downstairs on a stretcher and just as gently placed in the waiting ambulance.

Donna and Mario Garcia saw the young girl take her father's hand as the attendant closed the rear doors; then the ambulance, with red lights flashing and siren blaring, sped away.

"Let's go, Donna." Detective Garcia indicated his police car double-parked nearby. "I assume you want to be there with Captain Gavin."

"That's right." Donna got into the car with Mario. "I'm really worried, Mario. A stroke can be mild and the patient will recover fairly soon, or it can be a total, debilitating episode — complete paralysis. Then the patient can't speak or move — even feeding has to be done intravenously."

"How come you're such an expert? . . ."

Mario began, then stopped. "Of course, your mother — sometimes I forget she's a doctor." He looked at Donna sideways. "You know, you've got a jump on us sometimes, Donna. When your mother's a doctor and your father's a lawyer, you get to pick up all sorts of stuff that comes in handy — especially in criminal cases."

"Thanks, Mario — but don't put too much stock in it." Donna brushed her brown hair back off her forehead and stared through the windshield at the diminishing red lights on the ambulance, which was cutting through traffic and leaving them behind. Captain Gavin's official car led them in pursuit of the ambulance.

Mario deftly maneuvered the car through traffic. "The way you're acting, I'll bet you think Reilly has had a complete stroke, paralysis and all."

Donna said softly, "I think he's in a very bad way, Mario. I just hope he makes it." Mario looked down and saw Donna's fingers crossed in her lap.

"So do I." Mario turned grim-faced to the wheel and sought to close the gap between them and the speeding ambulance.

In the hospital waiting room, Donna and Mario waited patiently beside a very distraught Bonnie Reilly. At long last, a young doctor, wearing a plastic tag — RALPH BOVE, M.D. — came down the corridor to speak to them.

"Your father has suffered a serious stroke," he said to Bonnie. "His vital signs are at least stable at this moment."

"Tell me the truth, doctor. Will he be all right?" She looked at him with pleading eyes.

"There's no way of telling at this time," he said. "I'm sorry, but we can't even make a proper prognosis for at least twelve hours."

Detective Garcia took Bonnie in his arms again, while Donna drew the doctor aside and got the full story from him, just as Captain Gavin came over.

"So what I'm saying," Doctor Bove told them, "is that it will be quite some time before Mr. Reilly can communicate with anyone even when he regains consciousness. *If* he regains consciousness," he finished with a worried look.

Alone together, Captain Gavin told Detective Garcia and Donna, "Okay — that's it. We're going to have to work on the Roberts case without an assist from Reilly." He turned his attention to Donna. "Anything you turn up we'll be interested in, Donna. Go to it, but be careful."

"One question, Captain Gavin," Donna said as they walked to the exit door. "Do you believe Rick Roberts died an accidental death?" She waited for the tall, substantial-looking man to answer her.

"You want me to make an educated guess, is that it?" Captain Gavin said, half smiling. When Donna nodded, his face grew serious.

"All right, but please don't quote me. No, I don't believe it was an accident. I hate to say it, but Rick Roberts had a lot of enemies. There were plenty of people working for Rick Roberts who not only would've wanted him out of the way, they would've helped to do the job."

Mario Garcia dropped Donna off in front of her parents' house and said, "Now don't overdo, Donna. Stay home tonight and take it easy. Plenty of time for investigation tomorrow."

"Thanks for the ride, Mario," Donna said, and ran swiftly up the walk to the front door.

Inside, Donna saw a subdued Abbey and Jane sitting together in the living room. Spread out before them on the coffee table was a large scrapbook with clips of Rick Roberts. The book was Jane's; obviously she had run home to get it. Beside the scrapbook on the coffee table, a thin white candle was burning slowly; before it was a small vase with flowers. On the stereo, soft music was playing. Donna realized the two girls were staging a little memorial service of their own for Rick.

Abbey looked up and saw her sister. "It's all right, Donna," she said softly. "Jane and I have accepted it. I mean, it was awful, but we figure it had to happen. It was fate."

"Fate? How do you figure that?" Donna walked over and sat down beside them at the makeshift altar.

"Rick Roberts was too wonderful. Too good to live," Abbey said.

"Of course." Jane's lovely, wide blue eyes were dewy. "Handsome, talented, brilliant. An angel." She wiped a tear away. "He was too good to live. The good die young."

Donna suddenly remembered Captain Gavin's words. If the captain was right about how some people felt about Rick, these two kids were in for a terrific shock. Should she warn them? But they were, temporarily at least, comforted by their "good die young" theory. *I'll let them alone,* Donna thought.

"That's very thoughtful, the little ceremony you've arranged here," Donna said.

Abbey seized her sister's hand and squeezed it. "I knew you'd understand, Donna. I knew it."

"Hello, Donna. You're back at last." Donna looked up to see Pete O'Brien.

"You waited all this time, Pete?" Donna said. "You're terrific."

"Actually, they were in pretty bad shape," Pete said as they left the girls to themselves. "So I thought I'd hang around even after your folks showed up." He and Donna went into the dining room where Mr. Rockford and his wife were sipping coffee.

Dr. Rockford said ruefully, "I'm afraid there isn't much food left, Donna. I was busy at the hospital and . . ." She looked at her husband.

". . . and I underestimated the meatloaf," Mr. Rockford said.

Pete blushed. "My fault. I didn't know I was taking the last portion," he apologized to Donna. "Listen, I've got an idea. Why don't I take you to the Kabulah Cafe? I'll get you a souvlaki sandwich on pita bread. How's about it?"

"It sounds great, Pete," Donna said. She looked at her parents.

"Go ahead," her mother said. "We'll talk later tonight."

Fifteen minutes later, Pete drove Donna to the exotic Middle Eastern restaurant that was downstairs in a dingy, red brick building in a secluded section of the city near the water.

As they entered the attractive, tapestried room, haunting Egyptian melodies floated about the restaurant's guests, who sat cross-legged on huge pillows strewn around the floor. In each grouping, there was a low wooden table laden with food artfully arranged in separate dishes; diners were thoroughly enjoying the delectable meats and salads and wonderful pilaf rice dishes.

Donna and Pete made their way across the crowded, thickly carpeted floor to an arrangement of cushions and tables on one side of the room close to a small band of men and women, five in all, who were playing the romantic music on strange, stringed instruments and a brass timpani.

A waiter in a red bolero vest, high-necked white blouse, and red ballooning trousers gathered at the ankle, wearing Eastern slippers, flat with turned-up toes, took their order.

"My name is Hassan," he informed them.

"Oh, Pete, you couldn't have done a nicer thing tonight," Donna said gratefully, reaching over to kiss him. "I didn't realize until now how terribly tense I felt. But this" — she waved her hand at the lyrical little orchestra and the lush surroundings — "makes me feel new again."

Pete grabbed her hand. "Do you want to talk — or do you want to wait until after dinner?" He looked into her hazel eyes. "I get it. You want to eat. Go ahead."

Forty-five minutes later, Donna sighed with pleasure as she and Pete watched the waiter Hassan pour a fragrant herb tea into small, floral-printed cups. The waiter said to Donna, "You have enjoyed your meal, perhaps?"

"No perhaps about it, Hassan." Donna smiled warmly at him. "It was fantastic. Thank you. Now I can face real life again."

As they dug into the delicious baklava, a thin pastry filled with nuts and fruits and honey, Pete said, "What do you mean, real life? Anything I can do?"

"Maybe there is, Pete. With all that commotion at the studio today, it was hard for me to get an overall picture of what happened to poor Rick Roberts." Donna put her fork down on her plate and took a sip of the soothing hot herb tea. "If you have time, I'd like to go there now and take a real hard look at the whole setup."

"My pleasure, beautiful." With his easy,

athlete's agility, Pete rose from a cross-legged position to his feet in one swift movement. "I'll pay the check."

"Help," Donna said, holding out a hand. "I need a lift up."

In a moment Pete had pulled her up close beside him in unaccustomed and exciting nearness. In the dark room with the lilting, lovely melody of the band nearby, Donna felt irresistibly drawn to him. The people around them in the dimly lit room were involved in their own special intimacy, and it would have been so easy to respond to Pete's eager lips so near her own, but at that moment Hassan reappeared.

Donna knew Pete was as disappointed as she. It was hard not to encourage Pete but always when she did, she was sorry later. For one thing, she felt they were both too young and too uncommitted for a real love relationship, and for another, there were Donna's own unsettled feelings. Too often she was drawn in the same way to Mario Garcia. What kind of love could it be if you felt the same way toward two different young men? She was grateful that she didn't have to make any decision right now.

But when Pete and she got into the car for the drive downtown to TV Studio 13, he said, "Do you think we'll need more than an hour?"

"You don't have to wait for me, Pete, really you don't," Donna said.

"You know, I never hear you say that to Mario." Pete turned off the motor.

"What do you mean by that?" Donna said. Her heart began to race; she was fearful of what might come. Then it came.

"Things are different between us lately," Pete said. "And it's all because of Mario."

"I don't know what you're talking about," Donna said.

"Wherever I go, I see you with him. I haven't got anything against him personally." Pete's lips set grimly. "Mario's a nice guy — but I don't want him making passes at my girl."

Donna's cheeks flamed. "I'm not going to listen to any more of this. I can't believe you're saying it to me." She reached for the door handle, but Pete pulled her toward him.

"Don't," he said huskily. "Stay a minute and let's talk." His arms tightened about her and he tried to kiss her, but she gently pushed him away.

"Pete, I thought we agreed to take our time."

"I thought I'd break the agreement," Pete said. "Maybe my timing is off. . . . Listen, Donna, that guy Mario worries me."

"I'm getting out," Donna said as she opened the door. "I have to make a phone call."

She walked to the booth on the corner and dialed home. Her father answered the phone and Donna asked, "Dad, do you mind if Abbey takes a cab and meets me at Studio 13?"

"Not at all," Mr. Rockford said. "It's a great idea, Donna. The poor girl is really depressed. If you can use her in any way at all, it might help."

A moment later, Abbey was on the phone.

"I need you, Abbey. Can you take a taxi and be here right away?" Donna asked.

"You bet I can," Abbey said, her voice lifting three tones higher. "Wait for me!"

Donna rejoined Pete and they walked wordlessly to the front of the theater, where a door opened and Rex Vicente, the orchestra leader, was about to emerge. He had a sheaf of papers in his hand that he hastily shoved into his pocket.

"Oh! You're the girl who was backstage with the police today." He looked at Donna curiously.

"That's right," Donna said. "Mr. Vicente, could I speak to you inside a moment?"

"Sure. Sure." The orchestra leader stepped back into the softly lit entrance lobby and waited expectantly.

"From where I sat before the show, I heard Rick Roberts calling you offstage," Donna said.

"That's right," Rex Vicente said warily.

"Can you tell me what he wanted?" Donna asked carefully. "You don't have to answer, if you'd rather not."

"I don't understand what your interest is," Vicente said. His tone was gentle enough, but there was a strange expression on his face. Suspicion? Fear? Donna couldn't tell.

Pete came to the rescue. "In case you don't know, Mr. Vicente, this is Donna Rockford."

"Oh! I know who you are." He shook her hand. "Ask me anything you like."

He doesn't really mean that, Donna thought. *He's scared.*

"About why Rick wanted me," Rex Vicente continued quickly, "it wasn't anything important. He gets nervous — I mean he *got* nervous just before every show." Vicente cleared his throat. "You can't blame him. He was a perfectionist. Today he wanted me to, well, jazz up the orchestra." He smiled apologetically. "I don't want to blow my own horn, but they're quite a talented group of musicians. Rick — Rick didn't understand you have to be careful with creative people."

"Oh?" Donna looked at him, waiting.

"I don't blame Rick. Don't get me wrong. After all, he was the star." Vicente gulped. "The star calls the tune. I know that."

Donna said, "I don't want to keep you, Mr. Vicente." She looked at the sheaf of papers in his pocket. "I see you're working overtime."

Vicente looked bewildered, then patted the papers. "Oh, you mean these? They — they have nothing to do with 'The Teenage Talent Show.'" He looked distinctly uncomfortable. "This — this is personal."

"You've been very helpful." Donna shook his hand again. "Thanks a lot."

Rex Vicente left swiftly.

"He sure was glad to get away," Pete said as they headed into the studio.

"He acted guilty — as if we caught him at something. I wonder if we did, Pete."

The interior of Studio 13, so noisy and glowing with life only that afternoon, was now dark and still, like a huge electronic tomb. Through the gloom and stillness, Donna and Pete could see a small roped-off area onstage that marked the spot where Rick Roberts had met his end.

They walked swiftly down the aisle in the dark and mounted a short flight of steps that led to the stage when they heard a sharp *clank!* from somewhere in back.

"Oh, oh! We're not alone," Pete said.

"Let's have a look." Donna hurried across the stage.

They pushed aside the curtains that shielded the rear stage and saw a somewhat obese figure stooping over to pick something up from the floor. The figure straightened up and turned around, holding a small piece of something blue. It was David Gould, the audio man. His round, bearded, cheery face registered surprise, then broadened into a welcoming grin.

"Oh, it's you, Miss Rockford." David Gould came forward with outstretched hand. "Donna Rockford, girl detective. A pleasure to meet you." He shook Donna's hand briskly, as, with his other hand, he quickly inserted the blue fragment into the pocket of his jacket. "A pleasure."

"It's my pleasure, too," Donna said, barely refraining from asking him why he was hiding an innocent piece of something, unless it wasn't so innocent.

"You're probably wondering what I'm doing here," Gould volunteered. He edged them away from the equipment in the audio booth. "Well, I have an obsession about keeping my equipment shipshape. I've been in this business twenty years and you're only as good as your equipment. Maintenance is everything." He snapped off the light in the booth and led them out to the dark corridor. "I suppose you'll want to look around right on the set where Rick had the accident." He looked questioningly at Donna.

"That's right," Donna said, following him onstage with Pete and Abbey close behind. "Mind if I ask you a question?" When Gould nodded, she said bluntly, "Do you think it was an accident?"

"I don't know." David Gould was taken aback.

"Do you know if Rick Roberts had any enemies?" Donna looked searchingly at the bearded man's face.

The audio engineer's merry brown eyes sobered; he glanced nervously around, then seemed to come to a decision.

"All right, I'll tell you. I don't like to say anything about the dead, but it's probably going to come out anyway." His lips tightened. "Rick Roberts had plenty of enemies. And with good reason."

"What a terrible thing to say," Abbey said, as she came into the studio. "I don't believe it!"

David Gould looked at her pityingly.

"You're just a child," he said. "You'll learn different when you grow up."

Abbey reddened with indignation. "A child? Me? *Ohhhhhh!*" She moved away, over to Pete.

Donna said, "I'm afraid my sister is a little emotional right now."

"I don't blame her," David Gould said. "At times, Rick could be the nicest guy in the world. Well, I've got to be going."

When he left, Donna rejoined Pete and Abbey, who was still fuming.

"What a creep!" Abbey said. "He's just jealous of Rick!"

"Don't say that," Pete said. "He seemed like a nice man to me."

"To me, too," Donna said. "Listen, Abbey, just remember that Rick was only human. And human beings have faults, lots of them."

"Not Rick," Abbey said, slinging a lavender scarf around her neck, her dark eyes flashing. "He was perfect. Mr. Perfect!" Her voice broke again, and she bit her lip to keep from crying.

"Well, what have we here?" Donna said as they neared a backstage door marked RICK ROBERTS. PRIVATE. DO NOT ENTER! A huge red star was painted boldly on the door under the star's name.

"Not much the poor guy can do to keep anyone out now," Pete said, turning the knob of the door.

Rick Roberts' dressing room was very much like that of any show business person's

— a dressing table loaded with creams, lotions, brushes, boxes of tissues; floor-length wall mirror; lights for making up by; towels flung recklessly about; and a robe and some street clothes hanging on a coatrack.

But one item was outstanding — Donna noticed it instantly. A strong, musky aroma in the room. Heavy, seductive, distinctive. She remembered where she had smelled it — it was Lana Lawrence's heavily perfumed aura as she passed down the aisle earlier that day.

"What is it?" Donna turned to Abbey. "Do you know?"

"Not exactly. But it is Lana Lawrence's perfume," Abbey contributed. "I'll bet it's '*L'Amour Perdu.*' Lost Love. The world's most expensive perfume."

Donna lifted the top page of a small telephone memo pad that was half concealed by a box of facial tissues. She studied it a moment, then moved the page over to the lamp and peered intently at it. Then she shook her head.

"Here, Abbey, you've got eagle eyes. Can you make out what this is?"

Abbey came eagerly to her side and held the page closer to the bare bulb, squinting with the effort to see the impression on the pad. "Hmm . . . looks like *Stan* . . . *Standard* something . . . *Standard* . . . *Silver* . . . no . . . *Savings*? Maybe it's a bank. . . ." She turned to Donna. "What do you think?"

"A bank? Let me see. . . ." Donna squinted,

thought, and said, "That's not *'Savings,'* Abbey."

Abbey took another look and yelled, "*Savoy!* Is there a hotel? . . ."

"There is! The *Stanton Savoy!* You've got it," Donna said.

"It was my eyesight — but your brains," Abbey said. "Or was it vice versa?"

Pete and Donna exchanged glances. For the first time that day, Abbey's mood had lightened.

Footsteps sounded outside the star's dressing room. Donna opened the door and a dark figure appeared out of the shadows.

For a moment the man froze, then he stepped forward. It was Monte Clark. The tall, handsome, gray-haired announcer seemed surprised, but, true to his reputation for suavity, he broke into a charming smile.

"Ah! Donna Rockwell — and friends. Am I right?" He waited there and was about to continue when Pete broke in.

"The name is Rock*ford*," he said, stretching out his hand. "I'm Pete O'Brien, and this is the youngest Rockford of them all — Abbey."

The announcer shook hands with Pete and Donna, but when he came to Abbey, he held onto her hand. "I remember seeing you this afternoon, Abbey. You were in first row center, is that right?"

Abbey beamed. "Yes, I was! How did you know?"

"It's my business, Abbey, to notice as much as I can when I'm emceeing a show," he explained. "Not that anyone would have a problem noticing a beautiful young girl like you."

Abbey was enchanted. "Oh, Mr. Clark," she said, "wasn't it awful? Rick was so wonderful."

A film came over the announcer's eyes. He glanced at his wristwatch. "Can I help you? I don't have much time. . . ."

Donna said quickly, "If you could answer two or three questions, I'd really appreciate it."

"Go ahead," he said. "I hope I know the answers."

"Thank you, Mr. Clark. Here they are: Have you any idea how the accident happened? Is it possible that the rope breaking was deliberate? Maybe it was planned for someone else? Is there anyone you can think of who would have wanted to harm Rick Roberts?" She waved her hand. "I know. That's four questions. . . ."

"I don't have any answers, I'm afraid." The handsome announcer looked at Donna worriedly. Then a frown replaced his smooth social mask. "Rick Roberts is — was — an American institution, like baseball and apple pie. Only a deranged mind would think of harming a national hero like Rick."

Again he flashed an earnest look at Donna. "Why would anyone want to hurt him? As far as I know, Rick Roberts had no enemies. That's why I'm sure that those parallel bars dropped strictly by accident." He paused, then repeated, "Accident! It couldn't have been anything else. Now if you'll all excuse me. . . ." He grinned at them, then passed into the darkness as suddenly as he had appeared out of it.

Pete said, "What do you think, Donna?" following her back into the dressing room with Abbey close behind.

"I think Monte Clark was caught off base when he saw us here." She looked at her wristwatch. "It's not too late."

Abbey groaned. "Oh, no! What now?"

"It's time we got in touch with the Woman of Mystery," Donna said. "There are a few questions she'd better answer. The sooner the better."

She lifted up the receiver of a wall phone beside the dressing table, dialed a number, then said, "Hello, Stanton Savoy? May I speak to Lana Lawrence, please? . . . Oh, I see. . . . Listen, operator, I really have to talk to her. . . . When do you expect her back? . . . Oh, no! Well, thank you very much."

She turned to the others. "Now that's interesting," she said. "The operator says Lana Lawrence left early this morning, hasn't picked up any of her messages or phoned in for them — and she says there's a mountain of them. They don't know when — or if — she'll be back tonight."

"What's the next step?" Pete looked at his watch. "It's almost ten o'clock. I don't know about you two, but I'm beat. And I've got to be up at six to work out. The track meet is next Tuesday and this time U. of P. has to win."

"I'm exhausted," Donna admitted. "If you could drop me off at the dorm, Pete, and then take Abbey home. . . ."

"Please, Donna, can't I stay with you tonight?" Abbey said. "It's been a hideous day!"

"You bet." Donna surveyed her sister's pale face, with the unaccustomed dark circles beneath her eyes. "We can let the doctor and the lawyer know from my apartment."

Normally, referring to their parents like that was one of their favorite inside jokes, but Abbey didn't respond with even a glimmer of a smile.

At the front door of the dormitory apartment building where Donna lived, Mrs. Lerner, the housemother, met them with an eager smile.

"I'm so glad you're back, Donna," she said urgently. "Some man called you two or three times. I told him you were out, but he kept calling. He said it was *very* important and he had to speak to you."

"Who was it? Did he leave a message?" Donna asked.

Mrs. Lerner shook her head. "He wouldn't leave his name. He just said it's very, very important and he'd call back."

"Thank you, Mrs. Lerner." Donna hurried Abbey to the stairs. The housemother was alternately cranky or friendly. When she was friendly, like tonight, she was also extremely voluble. And Abbey was beginning to look worse with every passing moment. They trudged their way up the steep staircase to Donna's apartment on the second floor. As Donna opened the door, the telephone was ringing.

She sped across the room in the dark and picked up the phone. "Hello? Hello?" she said and waited. There was no answer. Whoever it was had hung up.

"Missed it." Donna snapped on the light.

For a moment, Abbey looked around as if not realizing where she was. Then she gave a little groan and threw herself into her sister's arms.

"Oh, Donna," she cried, "I feel so awful. I cried for hours; so did Jane. If I can help you figure out what happened," she looked pleadingly at her sister, "please give me a chance?"

Donna hugged her close. "You bet I will. You're such a sensational help, Abbey." Abbey's eyes lightened. "So many times when I get stuck on a case — and plenty of times when I don't — you come up with something fabulous that bails me out and I'm off and running again. We're a terrific team, babe."

"*You're* terrific." Abbey kissed her sister roundly on the cheek. "I feel better already. And I'm dead beat." She flung off her jacket, kicked off her boots, and sank down on one of the two studio beds.

At that moment the telephone rang again. As before, Donna sped to the phone and picked it up. But this time, someone was at the other end. The voice was deep and muffled.

"Donna Rockford?"

"Yes? . . ." Before Donna could ask who it was, the hollow-sounding voice said, "Lay off! If you know what's good for you, lay off the Roberts case. We'll get you and your sister if you don't!" There was a click at the other end, and the caller was gone.

"What was that?" Abbey asked.

Donna made an instant decision. "Wrong number," she said. No point in worrying Abbey. Poor kid had enough problems at this moment.

"Anything I can do for you? Get you something before I turn in for the night?" Abbey asked. Then, as Donna shook her head, she added, "*Uno* bowl of peanuts, maybe?"

Donna grinned. "My fatal weakness. They're in the cupboard."

Abbey got up and crossed over to the wall kitchenette. Donna hung up their jackets, then hastily undressed, slipped into her warm green bathrobe, and sat down in the bay window with the bowl of peanuts in her lap. She could not have said what it was that prompted her to pull the red curtains aside and look out into the darkness. At first all she saw was a shadow in the street below. But then it moved and she saw a figure in a raincoat — a man? a woman? If it was a man, could it be the one who'd just called? She shivered.

Abbey was now sound asleep. But Donna, shielded by the curtain, watched and waited until she saw the person, whoever it was, give one final look up at the apartment, then move quickly to a car further down the street, and disappear into the night.

Who was it? Donna wondered as she got into bed. Rex Vicente? Monte Clark, the announcer? Johnny Argyle? Bonnie Reilly? Bonnie was slim but almost as tall as either one of those men. Besides, shielded by the swaying boughs of a tree, the watchful figure was an indistinct blob more than anything else.

It could be anyone. Even David Gould. Even Lana Lawrence, wearing a bulky trenchcoat. Lana Lawrence. That was the name that meant the most to her right now. Tomorrow they would have to track the actress down. It seemed strange that she could be unavailable and had left no word at all at the hotel.

Tomorrow. She could hardly wait.

The Stanton Savoy was a beautiful, old turn-of-the-century hotel in downtown Philadelphia. As Donna and Abbey entered the elegant, chandeliered lobby and crossed the thick, floral Oriental carpets to the reception desk, they glimpsed a familiar figure in a high-backed red velvet chair against a pillar.

"Mario! What are you doing here?" Donna asked the red-haired young detective.

"Well, good morning," Detective Garcia said. "In answer to your question, Donna, I'm here for probably the same reason you are."

Before he could continue, Abbey said, "I'll bet. You couldn't wait to meet the glamour girl in person."

"Wrong. This is strictly police business," Mario said. But Donna noticed that his cheeks flushed.

"Of course, Mario dah-ling," Abbey said. "And the next bit of official business you'll need is to interview Lana personally. You'll probably have to take her out to dinner or a nightclub — all for the good of the police department."

"Cut the kidding, Abbey," Mario said as he got up from the chair. "It's time to check again."

"What do you mean?" Donna asked as they walked together to the clerk at the desk.

"I phoned up when I got here ten minutes ago but there was no answer. I figured maybe she was taking a shower. . . ."

"There's still no answer, Detective Garcia," the clerk said. "Go right up. I'm breaking the rules, but anything to help the police." He smiled.

"Thanks," Mario Garcia said tersely. "Follow me, girls. We're on our way to the fifteenth floor."

They stepped into a red-and-gold elevator with mirrored walls and were sped up to their destination. When they got out, they saw a blue-clad hotel maid wheeling a cart on which were suspended towels, brushes, and cleaning equipment.

When the maid heard what they wanted, she let Mario and the two girls into Lana's suite of rooms.

"I'm not going to make a search," Mario said. "For one thing, I don't have a search warrant. I'll just take a look around and hope Lana Lawrence comes back from wherever she's gone."

On an impulse, Donna said, "Excuse me a minute," and left before Mario could ask where she was going.

She ran out to the corridor and caught the maid just as the woman was rounding a corner. She looked up inquisitively as Donna approached.

"Yes? Can I help you?" she said suspiciously.

"You certainly can," Donna said. "I mean, if you would be good enough to help me." Donna indicated the big plastic trash bag on the side of the cart. "Did you empty Miss Lawrence's wastepaper basket this morning?" When the woman nodded, Donna said, "I wonder if I could just look? . . ."

The maid hesitated, then said, "Yes. Yes, you can. But please, do it fast."

Donna, surprised by the woman's quick acquiescence, hastily started to search the bag, when the maid said, "It's right on top, what was in the basket, Miss Rockford."

Donna looked at her with amazement. "You know me?"

The maid smiled. "My sister worked at the bank in Bayside — you know, the one where that Mr. Hudgins worked? Where that Mr. York took the money from the bank?" She added with authority, "You're the one who solved that case. My sister said you were terrific. She pointed you out to me one day in town."

Donna was embarrassed and pleased. "It's very nice of you to tell me all of that," she said, rummaging through the plastic bag.

She found an empty box of face powder marked "L'Amour Perdu" that Lana Lawrence obviously used with a lavish hand, as well as a ballpoint pen, dry, with lettering on it: BEVERLY WILSHIRE HOTEL, LOS ANGELES, and a sheet of paper headed DYNAMIC STUDIOS, HOLLYWOOD, CALIFORNIA. But the prize was a crumpled tissue that carried the very distinctive aroma of the perfume Lana Lawrence had worn yesterday. She sniffed it and then looked at the small pile of hotel stationery on the cart. The maid picked up an envelope and handed it to Donna. "You need this?"

"You've read my mind," Donna said and

stuffed the tissue into the envelope. "You'd make a pretty good detective yourself," she told the woman.

She hurried back to the room, where Abbey was triumphantly holding up a small oblong business card. "Look what I found! Marty Mazel's card. The most famous agent in Hollywood. I'll bet he's Lana Lawrence's agent, too."

Detective Mario Garcia picked up the telephone. "We'll see in a minute." He winked at Donna, who winked back. There was no doubt that Abbey — who had been badly shaken by the accident — was not grieving as she had once for the Russian dancer, Boris Dukov.

"Hello, operator?" Mario Garcia said. "Get me Marty Mazel in Hollywood, California, please." He turned to Donna and Abbey as the phone began to ring at the other end of the line.

"Hello . . . Mr. Mazel, please. . . . This is Detective Garcia of the Philadelphia homicide bureau. What's that? Yes, I'll hold. Hello? Mr. Mazel? I'm calling from the hotel suite of Lana Lawrence. What?" Mario Garcia's eyes registered surprise. "She's where? Yes, I understand. I'm in her suite at the hotel, but it's deserted. . . . London? That's incredible. Well, because she was at 'The Teenage Talent Show' yesterday when Rick Roberts . . . no, nothing like that. We're not accusing anyone, Mr. Mazel. I see. . . . Well, thank you."

He hung up the phone and said, "Miss

Lana Lawrence left for England at seven o'clock this morning by superjet — the Concorde SST, no less. Gone to visit friends until the end of the week, so her agent says."

"That's strange, isn't it?" Donna said. "I mean, dashing off like that?"

"It is. But there's nothing we can do about it for the moment," Mario said. "No point in hanging around here any longer."

As they got into the elevator, Donna asked, "Want to tell me what the police have as of this moment, Mario?" She leveled inquiring hazel eyes at him as they reached the lobby. "You don't have to tell me if you don't want to."

He brushed a gentle hand against her cheek. "Don't worry, beautiful. We haven't got a handle on anything yet. The minute we do, you'll be hearing from me."

"I appreciate that," Donna said, hiding her disappointment. "In fact, I'd appreciate anything, no matter how trivial it seems, Mario."

"I have a couple of names and addresses here that might interest you." Mario opened a small black notebook, ripped out a sheet, and handed it to Donna. "That's the address of the gofer's mother — Mrs. Argyle. I understand Rick did some terrific favor for her and her son Johnny. Go see her. Maybe you'll have better luck with her than we did."

"Thanks, Mario." Donna studied the paper. "Vicente . . . Gould. . . . Oh, Mario, you've even got the producer's address." She smiled at him. "You're a doll!"

He flushed, pleased, and said, "Can I give you two a ride somewhere?"

"Thanks, Mario," Donna said. "I think I'd rather walk."

As the young detective drove away, Abbey and Donna started to trudge through the downtown street. The early snowfall had stopped and was now a slushy, gray mess.

Abbey looked at her sister. "All right, tell Mother," she said. "Why are you brooding?"

"It's that Johnny Argyle everyone keeps talking about, the gofer. I hate that he's gone off somewhere on vacation and not told anybody where." She thought a moment. "Maybe we ought to go see his mother now. She's told the police she doesn't know where her son is. Let me think. . . ."

"Let's go see her," Abbey said. "Want me to give her a call and let her know we're coming?"

"No," Donna said. "Let's take the lady by surprise."

Mrs. Argyle was a dignified woman in her forties. She had a lean, spare body, but she supported herself with a cane as she opened the door a crack to see them. When Donna explained who she was and flashed her courtesy police card, Mrs. Argyle took the chain off the hook and let them in. She limped over to a rocking chair in the neat but poorly furnished living room and indicated a worn, upholstered blue sofa for them.

"Please excuse me for sitting here. I'm afraid that my hip isn't too good today, and I can't stand very long." She sat down in the rocking chair with great effort. "I had extensive surgery last year and I'm still not completely recovered."

"We won't take much of your time, Mrs. Argyle," Donna said. "It's just that there are a few questions about Rick Roberts. . . ."

"Dear Mr. Roberts!" Mrs. Argyle said quickly. "He was so good to us — so good." She saddened, remembering, then said piteously, "Isn't it terrible, his passing on so young?"

"That's why we're here," Donna said. "We're trying to learn as much as we can about him. Anything you can tell us could be a help in discovering why he died the way he did."

For the next twenty minutes, Mrs. Argyle gave the details of her illness, explained how Rick Roberts had come to her rescue, and, by the time she finished, tears came to her rather pale blue eyes and her voice had weakened. But Donna had not learned anything important, except that the Argyles, mother and son, had left Minnesota to come to live in Philadelphia when Johnny had been offered a job on "The Teenage Talent Show."

". . . because even though Johnny was excited by the idea of working on a big TV show, he didn't like the idea of living in Philadelphia," Mrs. Argyle said, smiling weakly. "Johnny hates big cities."

That gave Donna the opening she needed. "Your son's gone off on vacation," she said. "And the police say no one knows where he's gone, not even you. Is that true?"

Mrs. Argyle nodded and said brightly, "Johnny's just like his father. My husband always kept a mystery about a vacation until he came home. He loved the feeling of being free in the world, though to tell the truth, he never did anything worth keeping a secret about." She smiled fondly, remembering. "Of course he always called in once or twice while he was away."

"Do you expect to hear from your son?"

"I should think I'll hear from him," Mrs. Argyle said. "Especially after Mr. Roberts. . . ." Her handkerchief came up to her face again.

"I agree with you," Donna said. "Does Johnny always do that — I mean, go on vacation and not tell you where?"

"This is the first vacation the boy's ever had," his mother explained. "What with his father passing away four years ago, and then my getting so sick. . . ." She looked at Donna. "He's only nineteen, you know. Do you know Johnny?" She looked from one girl to the other.

"No. We're not connected in any way with the show," Donna said.

"I wish I could meet him," Abbey said

eagerly. "Think of all he must know about TV! I'm planning to go into the business some day."

And only yesterday she was going to be an astronaut, Donna thought. But she was grateful for Abbey's non sequitur a moment later when Mrs. Argyle leaned over and pressed Abbey's hand.

"Is that so? Well, then, you must meet Johnny as soon as he gets back." She started to get up. "Come with me, dear. I'll show you a picture of Johnny."

She took the two girls to a small room that was also sparsely furnished, but on the wall there were a few personal possessions of Johnny's. There was a brown-and-gold pennant lettered MARSHALL HIGH SCHOOL; a bulletin board with several notes, including one headed with the "Teenage Talent" logo and the notation WEDNESDAY 2:00 P.M. VOYAGE!; and several other items that Donna quickly read as Mrs. Argyle was indicating a picture on the wall to Abbey.

"This is Johnny's father." Donna left the bulletin board to join the other two. "He had an important position with the railroad," Mrs. Argyle continued proudly. The picture showed a quite handsome man of about forty, in a dark, somber suit and an earnest expression to match. "He was a supervisor," Mrs. Argyle continued. "But then he took sick and that used up everything we had, even the insurance." She felt the need to explain further. "I left everything behind with a dear friend in Minnesota when Johnny and I came East. I had to. I was coming here to the hospital and Johnny was starting a job."

As the woman rambled on, understandably sentimental, Donna took another look at the framed picture on the wall. From the nail on which it hung, there was suspended a small, curvy, pink plastic object hanging on a gray string. It looked odd, dangling atop the picture of Johnny's father, and Donna wondered what it was doing there, what possible meaning a seemingly useless little object like that could have for this young man she had barely seen and knew nothing about.

When Mrs. Argyle sighed, Abbey said, "You're tired, Mrs. Argyle. We shouldn't keep you like this." She looked at her sister accusingly. "We'll be going now, won't we?" Donna nodded agreement.

Minutes later, they were out on the street and Abbey turned on her sister. "What were you doing up there? The woman can't even walk without a cane. She's a widow who's still mourning for her poor husband — a man who lost his job and left her without a penny and then she lost their house and then she —"

"Stop!" Donna put her fingers to her ears. "One more word and I'll sell my car and give them the money." But she looked fondly at Abbey. "You're all heart, Abbey."

"And you're all head," Abbey said. "Disgusting, but it comes in handy sometimes. Did you get anything up there that you can use?" She broke off. "Uggh! Snowing again." A cloud rose from her breath. "I'm freezing!"

"Then let's get to the car, pronto. It's only a few blocks."

"Why did we have to park so far away?" Abbey wailed. "I may not make it."

"Abbey, let's start walking. I'll amuse you along the way."

"All right. Tell me everything you got out of Mrs. Argyle." Abbey skipped over an icy stretch of sidewalk. "And hurry, please, before I freeze to death."

"I've got to find Johnny Argyle. That's the number one priority."

"Why? I don't get it."

"I'll tell you why." Donna walked along, her eyebrows knit in thought. "I hate the idea the police thought up — that maybe Rick was deliberately killed. While a lot of people hated . . . didn't like him —" She looked up at her sister briefly. "I'm sorry, but it's true, Abbey. What I wish I could do is talk to the one person who might know what really happened. . . ."

Abbey, involved now, said, "Johnny Argyle? Lana Lawrence? No, don't tell me. Let me think." She punched her sister's arm. "I know. Howard Reilly, right?"

"Absolutely, Abbey." They were walking along a row of snow-covered hedges now.

"I hate to think that Howard Reilly could be the guilty one, Abbey." Despite herself, suddenly Donna was lost in thought. Abbey was running her hand through the light snow accumulating on the hedge, when all at once a heavy gloved hand flew out from behind the hedge and grabbed her wrist.

Abbey let out a blood-curdling yell just as a figure emerged from behind the hedge and reached for Abbey's bag with his free hand.

In that instant, Donna snapped out of her trance. She leaped at her sister's attacker, but an arm seized her about the throat and drew her backward. It was a second figure, smaller than the other, but strong. Both figures were wearing ski masks, and, in the outrageous onslaught, it was impossible to know if they were male or female. Even as Donna struggled to free herself from her attacker, she saw the other figure reach down to the ground, while still holding Abbey from behind, and pick up something.

It was a heavy chunk of something the size of a baseball bat, and, as Donna watched, the arm raised it high above Abbey's head and swung it fiercely downward.

That was all Donna needed — seeing the club about to bludgeon her sister.

She shrieked, "*Abbey!*" as sheer desperation helped her tear loose from her attacker. She leaped to her sister's side and grabbed the attacker's arm, deflecting the club in its downward path just before it hit its target. Instead, the club slammed the attacker's own shin bone with stunning force. The figure yelped and dropped the club, releasing Abbey.

Abbey let out a gleeful shout and cried, "Nice going, Donna!" then swung around to wade into her sister's attacker.

Now the battle was joined. Side by side the two girls battled with the other two. In the frenzy of the struggle, they were still unable to identify the sex of their opponents, whose heavy ski suits and ski masks were a most effective disguise.

Flailing away, Donna and Abbey were gasping for breath and definitely tiring when the unexpected happened.

Incredibly, the attacker who had held the club suddenly turned and started to run off. In the same moment, the second attacker ripped free of Donna's iron grasp and sped over to a driveway only yards away, disappearing into the blackness behind.

For a moment Donna and Abbey froze, too shocked to take action. Then the reason for the sudden retreat of the two ski-masked strangers became clear.

A police patrol car came tooling down the street and stopped. The doors swung open and a policeman spilled out of each side. One policeman ran directly to them and said, "What happened? Are you all right?" as he anxiously scanned their faces.

"Yes, yes!" Donna pointed down the street to where a figure was rounding the corner. But the second policeman was already in pursuit.

"The other one went that way!" Abbey yelled, indicating the driveway.

"Wait here!" the first policeman snapped back, as he hurtled onto the driveway and disappeared into the black night.

Donna and Abbey stood a moment in the

darkness, a heavier snowfall now shrouding them, enclosing them in a white-curtained closeness.

Silently they looked deep into each other's eyes; then threw their arms around each other and embraced.

"Oh, Abbey!" Donna said. "If anything had happened to you . . . I — I could have killed, I think."

"Me, too. But that creep took me by surprise." Abbey drew back and said, "Say, what's that you're pressing into my back?"

Donna took her clenched fist away from Abbey's back. It looked like the hand of a stranger. "I — I have no idea," she said.

"Then let's see." Abbey gently uncurled Donna's fingers. "Well, what have we here?"

In Donna's outstretched palm there rested a brass button. "I don't know where I got this," she said unbelievingly.

"You must have ripped it off that creep's jacket," Abbey said. "Look at the thread that's still on it. See how thick it is? Girl, that took strength."

"It took craziness. I was so out of my mind when I saw that club swinging at you. I guess I grabbed hold of this for support." She examined the button more closely.

"It's got an anchor on it, like seamen wear on their jackets," Abbey said. She was about to take a closer look when a voice spoke out of the darkness.

"He got away." The first policeman shook

his head disconsolately. "Nothing but backyards and fences there."

At that moment his partner came running toward them, his face almost comically alike in expression to his colleague's. "I didn't stand a chance of landing him, not in the snow, not on these streets."

All four got into the police car, where the cops took a look at the button Donna held. "Could be anyone," the first cop said. "Lots of men's clothes have those buttons. Did you get a look at their faces?"

"How could we?" Abbey said. "They had on ski masks. We don't even know they were men."

"The average mugger doesn't bother with ski masks," the cop said.

"And working in a pair like that, they could have had your purses and been gone before you knew what hit you," the other contributed.

Privately, Donna thought, *But were they muggers? And were they two men or two women or a man and a woman?* She had no way of knowing.

"We're taking you young women home," the policeman behind the steering wheel said. "Just to make sure nothing else happens to you tonight." He looked at Donna. "What were you doing out alone in a neighborhood like this, anyway? These streets aren't safe at night."

"The car!" Abbey said. "We forgot our car!"

"Show us where it is, and Ed here will drive it to your house," the cop said. "I'm making sure you get home safe."

Suddenly both girls felt very protected. They pulled up near their car, Donna gave the keys to the policeman named Ed, and, ten minutes later, they arrived at Donna's dormitory.

Out in front, a car was parked, with someone waiting beside it.

"Mario!" Donna said. "What are you doing here? How did you know?"

"I got the report on shortwave five minutes ago," he said. "Hello, Ed. Hello, Pat. I was just passing Eighteenth and Chestnut when I heard it. I figured it stood a good chance of being these two" — he looked at them, slightly annoyed — "and I figured it would be up to us on the force to bring them home safely."

"I don't get it," the policeman named Ed began.

"You will, sooner or later." Mario nodded his head toward Donna. "This is Donna Rockford."

"Say no more," Pat said. "I might have known. You're the girl that's always buzzing around headquarters, making waves," he said deprecatingly.

"Take it easy, Pat," Mario said. "Okay, she's just a teenager, but she's helped the department solve plenty of cases."

"You mean *she's* on the Rick Roberts

case?" Pat hmmphed. "She won't solve this one, Mario, my boy."

"Would you like to bet on it?" Mario began, when Donna cut him off.

"Would you men mind not talking about me as if I weren't here?" She turned to Mario. "Thanks for your help, but don't bet on me this time, Mario. I don't know anything at this point."

"I've got to hand it to you," the cop named Pat said. "It takes guts to say something like that."

The cop named Ed looked admiringly at Donna, then back at his partner. "I'll take that bet, Pat. This kid's got a pretty level head. How about five bucks?"

"You've got a deal," Pat said. "And now we'll say good night."

The girls left with Mario and went into the dorm. As they were heading upstairs, Abbey asked Mario, "I still can't figure out how you knew it was Donna and I who were in that mugging and how you knew to meet us here."

"Easy," Mario said. "The minute I gave that list to Donna earlier today, I figured she'd start running down as many people as she could." He waited while Donna unlocked the door and let them into her apartment.

"Then when the six-oh-eight call came in, from right near Johnny Argyle's house, I figured that that's where you two went." He sounded pleased with himself.

Abbey quickly deflated him. "Mario, dear boy, it's the kind of deduction that my brilliant sister comes up with all the time."

"Little girl, will you make yourself scarce?" Mario gently turned her toward the hallway. "I want to have a few minutes alone with the girl genius."

"Will you two please stop it?" Donna was annoyed. "Stop patronizing Abbey, Mario. And you," she turned to Abbey, "please don't call Detective Garcia *'dear boy.'* Show some respect."

"I can call you 'Mario,' can't I?" Abbey said flippantly, walking off. "How about 'Mr. Mario'?"

Mario walked further into the big sitting room, pulling Donna by the hand over to the bay window. The curtain was drawn and they were silhouetted clearly against it. Mario held Donna's wrist and drew her close.

"I was worried about you," he said.

Donna drew a hand across her forehead and said wearily, "I'm awfully tired, Mario. And I think Abbey and I had better get some sleep."

"Okay." He let her go and they walked back toward the door, where he bent down and kissed her on the cheek and said, "I'll talk to you tomorrow," and was gone.

Donna started to take off her jacket and stopped. Something made her walk over to the window. She pulled the curtain back and looked down to see Mario in the street, getting into his car. A moment later, he drove off. Then she noticed a car parked across the street. It was familiar, that car. As she watched, it slowly pulled away from the curb. She caught a quick look at the driver's face — it was tense and unhappy and drawn.

It was Pete O'Brien.

"Oh, no!" Donna gasped.

"No what?" Abbey came up beside her sister in time to see Pete's car pull away. "Omigosh! It's Pete!" She looked at her sister. "I'll bet he's angry enough to do anything!"

"Abbey, don't say that," Donna said miserably. "I can't worry about that now. I really can't!"

Abbey got their pajamas out of the closet and brought Donna's over to her. "Here you are, babe. Slip into these and get into bed. You need sleep."

Donna looked at the clock. Almost midnight. "You're right," she said. "No more sleuthing tonight." And she thought, *No more thinking about Pete, either. Or Mario.*

Abbey, closely tuned to her sister's feelings, said, "Just one last question, please. What are your plans for tomorrow? Tell me, or I won't sleep a wink."

Donna was in bed now. She looked at her sister fondly. "Tomorrow I want to take us to that new place that's just opened down here — the Mile-High Burger."

"That sounds great," Abbey said enthusiastically. Then she looked at her sister suspiciously. "Why would you want to do that? You hate junk food."

"Because," Donna said, snapping off the light, "I want to interview you in depth, Abbey. And you're always so much better with your mouth full."

"It figures," Abbey said. "Good night."

Donna reached across and squeezed her sister's hand. "And thanks for trying to take my mind off Pete."

Donna lay in the dark, thinking. Should she call Pete and try to explain how Mario had come to be here? She was too tired to do anything about it now. Like Scarlett O'Hara, she'd think about it tomorrow.

Her eyes closed and she began to drift off to sleep. In the dark she saw before her the faces of all the people from "The Teenage Talent Show" — from the script girl, Bonnie, to the producer, Abe Hazelkorn. And above all their faces she saw, superimposed, the face of Rick Roberts, his eyes closed as in a death mask.

Then from nowhere she saw the picture of Johnny Argyle's father and the strange, pink, wavy piece of plastic that hung above it. What was it?

"How about this?" Donna indicated a bright, orange-fronted, modernistic shop — the Mile-High Burger. She didn't have to wait for her sister's answer. Abbey was making her way to the entrance door, reading the sign in front aloud: WE GIVE YOU THE HAMBURGER — YOU ADD ALL THE FIXINGS! She turned to Donna. "This is for me. I can't wait."

The restaurant was filling up with the lunch crowd as Donna captured a table for two. "Go ahead, Abbey. I'll hold the seats."

She watched her sister cross quickly to the hamburger line, where a middle-aged man, obviously intrigued by Abbey's striking good looks, stepped aside and let her precede him. Then Donna saw her sister pick up the hamburger and walk to the fixings table. She watched in amusement as Abbey added an inordinate amount of trimmings to the hamburger bun, creating a hamburger that was now five inches high.

"Look!" Abbey, returning, gloated. "One of everything! The man behind the counter said it couldn't be done, but I did it!" She sat down with her creation. "Tomato, lettuce, pickle, cole slaw, cheese, bacon . . . oh, no, where's the bacon? Oh, here it is. Ketchup, relish, mayonnaise, secret sauce, onion. . . . I think that's all." Abbey looked at Donna. "Aren't you going to get your own lunch?"

"In a minute. I want to see you try to cram that thing into your mouth." She waited as Abbey daintily lifted the monstrous sandwich to her lips. Incredibly, she opened that pretty smiling mouth and somehow managed a gigantic, yet not unattractive bite, then chewed daintily away.

"You've convinced me," Donna said admiringly. "I'm going to get one of those for myself."

"Don't forget the barbecue sauce," Abbey called after her. "I forgot mine. Could you bring some back?"

Fifteen minutes later, Donna said to Abbey, "That was delicious. Now, tell me everything you know about Rick Roberts."

Abbey knew more about Rick Roberts than Donna had bargained for. She knew where he had been born — New Canaan, Connecticut; when he was born — 28 years ago; that his father was Rick Roberts, a famous actor who had dropped out of the public eye years before; but she did not know anything about his mother.

"Why not?" Donna demanded. "You know all about his father."

"His father was famous," Abbey said.

"You've told me a lot, but it isn't enough." Donna patted her sister's hand. "Don't mind me, Abbey. I'm just cranky because I can't get in touch with anything that could open up this case."

"I know what you mean. Rick was such a wonderful person." Abbey shook her head sadly. "I can't believe he's gone."

"That isn't what I meant, Abbey. I hate to keep reminding you, but there's more than a little evidence that Rick Roberts wasn't as perfect as you seem to think."

"I don't believe it! He was so good, so handsome, just like his father." Abbey continued, indignant, "If you don't think I gave you enough information, if you want to know more about his family, why don't you look it up like I did?"

"Where did you look it up?" Donna asked.

"Where else? The fan magazines," Abbey said. "Jane and I like to go down to the Fan Mag Shoppe and browse. Sometimes we stay for hours. We can't afford to buy the old copies."

Donna jumped up from the table. "Abbey, you never fail me! You've given me a place to start."

"I have?" Abbey gathered up her things.

Donna started for the door with Abbey. "Where's this fan mag place?"

"Follow me," Abbey said, pushing through the doorway. "But I still don't get it. Why are you so happy?"

"I want to learn everything I can about Rick Roberts, Senior," Donna said. "You know what they say: 'Like father, like son.' That's the key, Abbey! I feel it in my bones."

SIX

Two hours later, Donna and Abbey were seated on the floor in the family room at the Rockford house. Spread about them was a multicolor mélange of magazines, posters, and assorted show business literature.

Abbey smiled gleefully as she looked up from a fan magazine she was reading. "I really took you for a bundle, didn't I?"

"I don't mind," Donna said, "provided we turn something up. So far, nada."

At that moment, the telephone rang and Donna hurried to it. It was Mario Garcia, sounding solemn.

"Donna, I just want to tell you that the funeral is tomorrow morning at ten o'clock at the Park Vendome funeral parlor. You'll want to be there, right?"

"Right, Mario. Thanks for the information." Then she remembered. "Mario, what have the police done about Lana Lawrence?"

"S.O.P. — Standard Operating Procedure. I've got a call in to London right now." He paused. "Don't trouble your pretty little head about it. . . ."

"If you say that once more, Mario, I'll take you off the case." It was their inside joke, but Mario got serious.

"Be careful, Donna." Mario's voice dropped. "I don't like this case."

"Neither do I. Don't worry, Mario. I'll be careful." As Donna hung up, Abbey looked at her appraisingly.

"He's really got it bad, huh, Donna? How does it feel to have two men panting for you at the same time?"

Donna sat down on the floor cross-legged beside her sister and picked up a magazine. "Quit kidding around, Abbey. We've still got a pile of these to go through. It's all junk." Unhappily, Donna thumbed the pages of the magazine.

A few minutes later, their mother, Dr. Rockford, came in, shaking snow from her jacket.

"This is a pleasant surprise, Donna." She kissed her daughter. "You're staying for dinner, I hope?" When Donna nodded, she waved her hand to the strewn-about papers.

"What's this? Hmmm . . . screen magazines, TV? Oh, I'll bet it's research on Rick Roberts." She bent down and picked up a copy of *Photoplay*, dated some twenty years earlier.

"Oh, this is fascinating! I remember reading these when I was just about your age, girls." She turned the pages and stopped at a picture of Rick Roberts, Senior. "Here he is, Rick Roberts. What a crush we had on him — he was like Scott Baio and Tom Selleck rolled into one." She stopped. "What's the matter, Donna? You look discouraged."

Donna sighed. "I am. We've spent lots of money and most of the afternoon and we've found *nothing*." She tugged at a strand of her long brown hair. "I wouldn't care, Mom, but this is the kind of case where there isn't much I can do that the police can't do better." She slapped the magazine. "Except for something like this. If only I could pick up *something*. . . ." She sighed again.

Abbey jumped up from the floor and said dramatically, "This is all too, too depressing! What we need is food, and laughter, and something to eat, and some recreation, and maybe some cheese snacks? . . ." She looked at her mother, who nodded. Abbey grabbed a magazine. "Wait and see, Donna! Have I got a surprise for you!" She stopped and kissed her mother on the cheek. "Don't forget the cheese snacks, Helen, and toss in a couple of English biscuits, will you, dear?" Then she sped up the stairs.

Dr. Rockford turned back to Donna. "I know how you feel. Those magazine stories are full of invented nonsense. But every now and then we used to get a hot blind item from a gossip column." She stopped. "Why are you looking at me like that?"

"The gossip columns!" Donna slapped her forehead. "*That's* what we should have been reading!" She beamed at her mother. "Mom, what's a blind item?"

"Oh, you know, a reference to a big star, not naming him by name, but dropping a juicy bit of gossip. Like, 'What big Western cowboy hero is splitting with his wife after twenty years of marriage because he's gone ga-ga over a blond go-go dancer?' " Both mother and daughter broke into laughter.

Donna said, "You're too much, Mom. I love you madly, and as my darling sister just said, Helen, I'm starving." She hugged her mother and fell down on the sofa next to a pile of magazines. "The gossip columns — of course!"

"I'm a slave to my children," her mother said, hurrying out, pleased that Donna was in good spirits once more.

Donna dug into the magazines again, concentrating on the gossip columns, when the front door bell rang. She opened the door to see Pete O'Brien stomping snow off his feet on the doormat.

"Am I welcome?" He looked anxiously at Donna. "Or am I interrupting something?"

Donna took him by the hand and pulled him inside, which was a mistake. Pete drew her toward him, held her close, and said, "Oh, Donna, let's not fight." He put his hand behind her head and kissed her, unaware of her feelings at the moment.

"Please don't, Pete," she said, slipping out of his arms. "I'm in the midst of something — and you could help."

Pete sighed and said, "Sure. But when this case is over, you and I are going to have a serious talk." He looked her directly in the eye. "About you and me. And about Mario Garcia. . . ."

"Oh, don't start that, Pete. Not now." She led him to the sofa and handed him a magazine, *Screen Gems.*

"You want *me* to read this slop?" he asked.

"Please, Pete. I need all the help I can get. Take this box of clips and put a clip on every gossip column, so I can run through the pages real fast and dig up what I can about Rick Roberts and his father."

Seeing Donna's desperation, Pete said, "Okay. I'll do it."

For ten minutes the two of them pored over the magazines, when they suddenly heard a fanfare from upstairs and Abbey yelled, "Hold everything! A star is born!"

At that moment, Dr. Rockford came in through the doorway, carrying a tray of snacks, so she, too, saw the apparition coming down the steps.

It was Abbey, all right, but skillfully disguised and made up. She wore a blond wig, a white, form-fitting evening gown that stopped just above her ankles; she had penciled in arched eyebrows and added thickly crimsoned lips, while from her ears there dangled three-inch rhinestone earrings. She stopped at the bottom of the steps, threw her head back in a perfect imitation of that famous sexy smile, that infectious giggle, and said, in almost the identical half whisper, "Hi! Do you know who I am?" There was no mistaking it. All three spoke practically at once.

"*Marilyn Monroe!*"

"You're terrific, Abbey," Pete said. "Even I recognized you. And what I don't know about old-time movie stars is unbelievable."

Abbey held up a magazine with a full-page picture of Marilyn Monroe dressed almost exactly like she was. "I used this as a model," Abbey said. "What's the matter, Donna?"

"Let me have that!" Donna reached for the magazine and read the opposite page. Her eyes widened in surprise. "It's here! I can't believe it, but it's here!"

Abbey dropped her Marilyn Monroe pose. "What are you talking about? You're ruining my big moment."

"Right in Kitty Kenway's column!" Donna held up the page. " 'What hotshot teenage idol — connected to a *railroad?* — was très unpopular way back when he was in that very special high school in New York City for talented kids? That item in the yearbook when he graduated, plus his miserable actions on his show, is enough to lose him a couple of million fans. *Tch tch.*' So the big TV idol has feet of clay after all."

"What does that mean?" Abbey asked.

Donna pointed to the paragraph. "Don't you see? 'Railroad' — those initials are *RR.* I think she means Rick Roberts."

"I don't believe it," Abbey said, sounding unsure.

"It's all here, Abbey. 'That very special high school.' It's probably the High School for Theater Arts."

"That's right," Abbey admitted. "Rick spent part of his life in New York. Gee, I wonder what it means."

"Don't worry," Donna said. "We'll find out. Rick's funeral is tomorrow morning. It should be over before noon. I can take a train to New York City and be at the High School of Theater Arts by two-thirty and see what it's all about."

It was a relaxed group that sat down to eat a half hour later. When dinner was over, Pete pushed back his chair. "That was a sensational meal. Thanks a lot." He smiled at the girls' parents.

"You're pale, Donna," Dr. Rockford said. "So's Abbey. Why don't you both go out and get some air?"

"Good idea." Pete pulled Donna up. "Come on! We'll build a snowman."

"You'd better say 'snowperson' or she won't go," Abbey said.

A few minutes later they were into their boots and outer clothing while Donna surveyed her sister, who had thrown a jacket over the white evening dress, put on a pair of hip boots, jammed a flapped hunting cap of her father's over the blond wig, and was preparing to go outside with them.

"You can't be serious," Pete said to her. "That outfit!"

"She's serious," Donna said. "Come on."

Outside, dusk had already turned to night. Across the street a compact gray car started up its motor and raced away in the dark.

Donna said, "Who was that?"

Abbey grabbed her sister's arm. "Forget it, Donna. We need a break." She kicked a pile of snow together in one spot on the front lawn and said, "There! That's the base of the statue." Within seconds, Pete, Donna, and Abbey were pasting huge globs of packed snowflakes onto the snowman. Fifteen minutes later, incredibly, they were putting the big round head onto its shoulders. Abbey stuck a large carrot lengthwise in the face for a ludicrous orange nose, and Pete tipped an old felt hat of Mr. Rockford's on its head, while Donna dug beneath the snow-covered hedges for some stones for eyes. It was as she stooped behind the hedge that the gray car came around the corner, about to pass the Rockford house again. It slowed down just as it neared them. Donna was trying to make out the letters on the license plate when it happened.

"Aha! Gotcha!" The yell came from Pete, and, with a *swoosh,* a good-sized snowball hit Donna between the shoulders.

Donna yelled, "Pete! Abbey! Of all the times to play games. . . . You're hopeless!"

"Why are you so interested in that car?" Pete asked. "It's just a car. No big deal."

"I don't agree," Donna said. "Someone's boon hanging around, at my place and now here." She shook her head slowly. "I don't like it."

"I know that look," Abbey said. "She's going to come up with something."

"I know," Pete said. "And I wish she wouldn't." He groaned and chucked Donna under the chin. "Why did I have to fall for a brain like you? Will you tell me that?"

Donna said suddenly, "Howard Reilly. Of course!" She turned to Abbey. "Come on. Let's go in and you can change into something respectable. We're going visiting."

"Where are we going?" Abbey asked as they headed up the walk. "Can't it wait until morning?"

"No, it can't," Donna said.

Pete waited until Abbey disappeared into the house and then he grabbed Donna by the arm. "Don't rush off, Donna," he said, putting both arms around her. In the next instant, he kissed her.

Donna pulled away. "Pete! Why are you coming on to me all the time? Can't you see I have things on my mind?"

"Yeah, and I know what they are." He pointed a finger at her. "Mario Garcia. Admit it!"

"You're nuts — and I haven't got time to argue with you." She turned and yelled over her shoulder, "Good night!" without looking back as she entered the house and slammed the door. *It serves him right,* she thought.

SEVEN

As Bonnie Reilly opened the door of her apartment, she was stifling a yawn. "Excuse me," she said. "I was asleep. Come in." She looked slightly rumpled in a short blue housecoat.

"I'm sorry we didn't call before we came over," Donna said, taking off her coat.

"Here, I'll hang that up," Bonnie said. She took their coats from them in the hallway. "You can go into the living room. I'll be right with you."

The two girls entered the small, conventional living room, decorated in shades of beige and brown and rust. They both sat on the tailored tan sofa, and Bonnie came in and took a brown chair near the hallway.

"I was asleep," she said. "I spent the morning at the hospital with my father. Then they said I had to leave. It was only two o'clock, but I was exhausted." She looked at them wanly. "I couldn't sleep a wink last night. So I just came right home from the hospital and fell into this deep sleep."

"I'm sorry we disturbed you," Donna said, apologizing again. "How is your father?"

"There's been no change," Bonnie said.

"That's too bad," Abbey said. "I know how I'd feel if it were my father. I think you're very brave."

Bonnie cast her a look that was totally devoid of emotion. Then she turned to Donna. "I'll try to answer any questions you want to ask me. I guess that's why you're here." Bonnie got up restlessly and went to the window, where she pulled back the curtain and said, "Oh! It's snowing! How long has that been going on?"

"It started about four o'clock this afternoon," Donna said.

"No, four-thirty," Abbey corrected her. "I know because it was just when we got back to the house that I looked at my watch."

"I'll take those questions now," Bonnie said, sitting down across the room from Donna.

"I realize how tired you must be, Bonnie, so I'll make it brief." Donna crossed her legs. "You and Johnny Argyle? Is it true that —"

"That we were going steady?" Bonnie said quickly. "Yes, it's true."

"Well, have you told the police where he

went on vacation?" Donna paused. "Do you want to tell me?"

"I wish I could," Bonnie replied, "but I haven't the slightest idea."

"Really? You mean, he just took off on a vacation without telling you where he was going?"

"That's right," Bonnie said.

"But he's your boyfriend!" Abbey cut in.

"Right. But that's the way Johnny is." She smiled. "He wanted to go off on a trip and not let anyone — not even his mother — know where he was going."

"Can't you even *guess* where he might be?" Abbey asked.

"I wouldn't even try," Bonnie replied. "He could be anywhere. I know that sounds weird, but that's the way it is with Johnny and me." Her mouth lifted in a half smile. "We like to hang loose."

"Can you tell me what Johnny's relationship with Rick Roberts was?" Donna asked.

"Well, as you know, Johnny is the gofer on the show. And, he is — was, nuts about Rick." Bonnie seemed to be searching for the right words. "As a matter of fact, Johnny is just about the only person on the entire show who really liked Rick."

Abbey drew in a shocked breath. "What? How can you say that?" Abbey's face was flushed. "Everyone in the world loves Rick Roberts."

Bonnie cast Abbey a sympathetic look. "You can't really believe that," she said softly.

"Everyone has faults. And, believe me, Rick Roberts had plenty."

"Leaving that aside for the moment" — Donna flashed a warning look at Abbey — "I mean, assuming that Rick Roberts wasn't the god everybody thought he was — and assuming that he had plenty of enemies as most famous people do —" She broke off. "Why was Johnny so devoted to Rick?"

Bonnie's response was unexpectedly candid. "Johnny's a nice guy, but he's a child in some ways. I mean, he's one of those people who hates to believe there's no Santa Claus." She made a little face. "With Rick Roberts, he sure had a wrong number."

"Why?" Donna demanded. "Did Rick Roberts treat him better than the other people on the show?"

"No, he wouldn't know how to treat anyone under him decently," she said scathingly. "Rick Roberts had the worst power drive imaginable. That's why everyone hated him!"

Donna said gently, "Bonnie, I know you're upset, but there's no reason to lose your temper." As Abbey looked gratefully at her, Donna continued. "Can you tell me why your boyfriend was so devoted to Rick?"

Bonnie sighed. "Okay. I'll try to keep it cool. It all happened about a year ago, when Johnny and his mother lived in Minneapolis. They were in pretty desperate shape at the time." Her face softened. "Johnny's mother has a very serious heart condition and to make things worse, they were about to be evicted from their home. The situation was hopeless, until Mr. Wonderful" — she corrected herself — ". . . until Rick Roberts came to their rescue with a check for ten thousand dollars."

Donna leaned forward. "I'm really impressed, Bonnie. That was a very decent thing to do. Unless there was some reason. . . ."

"You bet there was," Bonnie said quickly. "You see, the show was just getting off the ground, and Rick was beginning to get rotten word of mouth in the trade. I mean, his character was showing." She looked at Abbey and nodded her head sympathetically. "So the PR people dreamed up a big publicity stunt. Before the show's ratings could drop any more, they thought of something to improve Rick's image. He would be the Great Humanitarian."

"What made Rick pick Johnny Argyle's family?" Abbey asked, unable to restrain her curiosity.

"Rick was getting lots of fan mail by then. A good part of it, like any other fan mail, included requests for help. You know the kind — people need a job, or money, or all sorts of things." She shifted in her chair. "So the PR department threw all the letters asking for help into a big box and Rick picked one out. The one he picked was a letter written by a friend of the Argyles."

"I see," Abbey said softly.

"Well, that check for ten thousand helped pay the mortgage on the house and then provided Johnny's mother with one of the best heart surgeons in this country. That operation saved her life. And, to top it off, Rick gave Johnny a job on his show." She looked at Abbey. "The papers were full of it."

"I remember," Abbey said. "It just seemed like one of a hundred wonderful things about Rick."

For some reason, Donna felt terribly frustrated. While Bonnie spoke with apparent frankness, Donna felt an undercurrent. Of what? Did she know more than she was telling? And if so, what? From the moment they had walked into the apartment, Donna had felt that Bonnie Reilly, while being overtly friendly, although sleepy (and was the sleepiness real? or just a pose?), was holding something back. What was it? She had to find out.

She managed to catch Abbey's eye. "Bonnie, excuse me. *Do* you *have* a bathroom off the hall?" Before Bonnie could answer, Donna got the nod from Abbey, meaning, *I get the message. I'll do it.* It was an answer to Donna's signal. Whenever either one signaled two words beginning with the initials "D" and "H," it meant "*D*ivert *H*im, or *H*er." When Donna strongly accented the two words in her question, Abbey was instantly alerted.

As Bonnie rose and said, "I'll show you

where the bathroom is," Abbey instantly pointed to the drawn beige draperies over the windows.

"Oh, where did you get these?" Abbey said. "I've been looking all over town for something just like them."

As Bonnie turned back, Donna said, "Don't bother. I'll find it myself," and quickly left the room.

"I got them on sale at Shelby's," Bonnie was saying to Abbey as Donna stepped into the hallway.

In the hall, Donna quickly pulled open the first door, which turned out to be a closet. She reached a hand into the clothes hanging there, then quickly shut the door and walked down the hallway to the bathroom. When she came back just minutes later, Bonnie looked at her wristwatch. "Oh, it's getting late. I hate to cut this short, but . . ."

"Of course. We understand." Donna got up from the couch. "We won't take up any more of your time."

Donna noticed a picture on the wall, of a girl at a microphone, with a man coming up behind her.

"That's you, isn't it, Bonnie?" she said.

"Yes. After one show, I went to a mike to try it — I love to sing. Dad . . ." she broke off and gulped. ". . . Dad took my picture." Her voice grew bitter. "That shadow is Rick. He took the mike out of my hand and told me never to do that again."

Donna and Abbey glanced at each other.

In the front hall, Bonnie gave Donna and Abbey their coats. Donna put her arm into a sleeve of her jacket and said, "Bonnie, you'll let us know if you hear from Johnny, won't you?"

"Oh, yes," Bonnie said. "I'll let you know the minute I hear from him." Bonnie showed them quickly to the door and said good night without looking at them.

Outside at the elevator Abbey said in a low voice, "Did you get anything?"

"Something very interesting," Donna said.

"Tell me! What?"

"Not now," Donna murmured. "Wait till we get back to my place."

As they entered the elevator, Donna looked back at the door to Bonnie Reilly's apartment. Just before the elevator door closed, Donna heard a click from the hallway. Did she imagine it or was Bonnie watching them through the peephole? That was what the click sounded like — a peephole shutter snapping open.

A half hour later, they were in Donna's apartment. Abbey opened her tote bag and took out a pair of black-and-orange satin Japanese pajamas. She shoved a bowl of peanuts onto her sister's lap and said, "All right — spill!" Then she sat down beside Donna in the red-cushioned bay window. "And by the way, do you mind telling me why you made me wait a half hour to hear what you found out tonight?"

"I needed time to think about everything Bonnie said and glue it into my head." Donna cracked a peanut and popped it into her mouth. "And also, you know how I love to get your opinion right out of the blue." Abbey was pleased. Donna went on, "You remember when I took that trip to the bathroom? Well, I accidentally on purpose opened the wrong door — and discovered that Bonnie Reilly lied to us."

"She did?" Abbey's dark eyes glittered. "I'll bet she lied about Rick, too!"

"I don't think so, Abbey. Please let me finish." Abbey nodded. "Bonnie said she hadn't been out of the house since three o'clock this afternoon. But it started to snow at four-thirty, right? Well, what I found in the closet, way in back of our two coats, was a jacket wet all over the shoulders. Not damp, Abbey. *Wet.* Which means that little Bonnie Reilly came into her apartment only a very short time before we got there."

"Wow!" Abbey registered disbelief. "Then that whole yawning routine was an act?"

"Exactly. And that means that maybe she was the one hanging around our block when we were having dinner."

"And when we went outside and built the snowperson. . . ." Abbey gasped. "Could she be the one who tried to conk me?"

"She's not the criminal type," Donna said, frowning. "Why should she want to hurt you, Abbey? It doesn't make sense."

"It doesn't," Abbey said.

Donna chewed a peanut thoughtfully. "Why is she lying to us? That's what I've got to find out."

Abbey stood up and yawned delicately. "You do your thing, Donna, and I'm going to do mine — sleep. I'm beat." She bent down, kissed her sister, and got into bed.

Donna sat quietly in the bay window, looking out at the darkened street. Tonight there was no one outside monitoring their apartment house as someone had done the night before. Who was it who had stood there in the darkness looking up at this very window? Was it the mysterious man caller? She hated to think such a thing, but the thought would not go away. Could it have been. . . . She tried to dismiss the ugly thought. He had seemed like such a nice young man and he had had more of his share of trouble already. But she wondered: Was it possible that he hadn't left Philadelphia at all? Was it possible that the one watching their apartment was Johnny Argyle?

She got into bed, but sleep didn't come easily. As the clock ticked away by her bedside, she thought about Bonnie Reilly. Did Bonnie know where Johnny Argyle was? If she did, why was she lying?

And what about Rick's death? Did Johnny have anything to do with it? Did Bonnie's father?

Or did Bonnie *herself*?

The snow covering Whispering Knoll Cemetery was beginning to melt under a warm sun by eleven o'clock the next morning.

As the mourners congregated in front of the newly dug grave that had been prepared to receive the mortal remains of Rick Roberts, Abbey whispered urgently to her sister.

"Donna, you should have listened to me. Look, everyone's dressed in dark clothes."

"But not in black, Abbey. And why should they be? It's not as though we're members of Rick's immediate family." She surveyed her sister, who was wearing a black mourning ensemble she had put together especially for the occasion.

"Really, Donna," Abbey said. "Sometimes

your lack of sensitivity truly amazes me. I'm just trying to show a little respect, that's all."

"Okay," Donna said. "I'm sorry I mentioned it."

They moved into the semicircle of people surrounding the graveside, where Donna could observe the principal mourners.

A stoop-shouldered, fidgety Rex Vicente was studying a patch of snow on the ground, while beside him stood Bonnie Reilly, looking sullen. Next to Bonnie was David Gould, somber-faced.

A TV mobile crew, about twenty yards off, was already recording the scene for that night's edition of the "Six O'Clock News."

Abe Hazelkorn, the show's producer, was conversing quietly with the director of the TV crew; off to one side, newspaper photographers were busily snapping away.

"Everyone from Rick's show is here," Abbey said, sighing.

"Not quite," Donna said. "I don't see Monte Clark anywhere."

Abbey searched the crowd carefully. "Right. He's not here. I wonder why."

Just then, Detective Garcia came over to them. He greeted them and said, "What's worrying you, Donna?"

"We were wondering why Monte Clark isn't here."

"Abe Hazelkorn told me Clark has a very bad cold and has to tape a show this afternoon." He looked at Donna. "Are you thinking what I'm thinking?"

"Yes, Mario." Donna shook her head. "It's a pretty weak excuse for not showing up at a funeral."

"You've got it," the young detective said. "He was due to come in for questioning this morning. Now we have to delay it until tomorrow. Very convenient, catching cold."

Abbey nudged her sister. "Will you take a look at that?" She indicated a taxi that had pulled up on a snow-covered mound in the roadway about fifty yards away. The rear door opened and a slim woman, dressed in black and wearing a heavy black veil, got out. She ventured only a few feet away from the taxi, then stopped and stood alone and unmoving, watching the group around the grave.

"The Woman in Black!" Abbey said excitedly. "Like the one that goes to Rudolph Valentino's grave every year!"

But Donna's attention was directed elsewhere. From the corner of her eye, she saw David Gould making a furtive move as he stood next to Abe Hazelkorn. It all happened in an instant. Had David Gould slipped something secretly to the producer? She wished she hadn't missed it.

At that moment, a black-robed minister arrived at the graveside, quietly opened a Bible, and began to intone solemnly the familiar words of the funeral service.

When he finished, Abbey tapped Donna on the shoulder. "Look over there! Do you believe it?"

Donna looked at the rise in the roadway, where the taxicab was waiting and saw the black-clad woman disappear inside. Then the cab sped away on the snow-covered road.

"What a weird way to behave! Why all the mystery?"

"I wonder if any members of Rick's family are here," Donna said.

Mario Garcia said, "Not one, Donna. We stopped everyone at the gate and had them identify themselves. No family members present. How do you like that?" He checked his watch. "I'm heading back to headquarters. Can I give you two a lift?"

"I appreciate that, Mario," Donna said. "I've got a lot of studying to do."

"I thought we were going to New York City," Abbey said.

"We'll have to put it off till later in the week." Donna took her sister's arm as they walked to Mario's unmarked black police car.

"What's bothering you now?" Abbey asked.

"Just something I saw back there. . . ."

Detective Garcia asked, "What was it, Donna?"

Donna hesitated. She remembered the plump David Gould as a gentle and, on the face of it, decent man. She didn't want to get him into trouble, if she could help it.

"Forget it," Donna said to Mario. "It's probably not important."

In the car, she thought, *I hope it isn't important. But I've got to find out what David Gould was up to back there.*

"Don't forget that we want to see the six o'clock news," Donna said. "Maybe someone on the TV crew got a shot of the Woman in Black."

The two girls were in Donna's apartment. A fire in the grate had taken the chill off the room, and both girls had been studying hard ever since Mario had dropped them off at one o'clock.

"Can't we eat now?" Abbey asked plaintively. "My stomach is growling so loud I can't hear myself think." She slammed her history book closed, got up from the desk, and strode toward the kitchenette, "Pork lo mein, here I come!"

Moments later, with a delicious aroma emerging from the Chinese takeout dinner Abbey had insisted on bringing home with them, Donna looked up wearily from her own studies and said, "You win, Abbey, or at least the lo mein does. It smells fiendishly fantastic."

Within minutes, both girls were sitting in front of the TV set, digging into the luscious Chinese food, Abbey, of course, using chopsticks.

"Right on time!" Abbey said, indicating the clock on the wall with her chopsticks. "It's one minute to six. Here comes the news. . . ."

"Okay, Abbey. Don't you want a fork?"

"Peasant." Abbey daintily lifted a morsel of pork to her mouth. "Chinese food requires chopsticks." Then, as a succulent piece of meat came to her lips, it dropped onto her lap.

"Now who's the peasant?" Donna said, laughing.

"Sssh, here it comes," Abbey said.

Theme music swelled up from the TV set and the bold title "Six O'Clock News" flashed on the screen. Then a handsome duo appeared on screen — the news team: a lovely, young black woman and a Hollywood-type blond young man.

"Good evening," the young man said. "The news is very sad tonight. Philadelphia today laid to rest a star known throughout the world for his youth, his talent, and his charm."

"I still can't believe it," Abbey said, laying down her unfinished eggroll.

"Rick Roberts began life in an aura of stardom," the female newscaster said. "His famous father, Rick Roberts, Senior, was a prominent Hollywood star in the nineteen-forties and fifties."

On came film clips of Rick as a child playing with his father on the lawn of their Beverly Hills home. Then violins took over the soundtrack as videotape coverage of the funeral came on the screen.

There were shots of various celebrities, movie stars, and TV personalities — as well as local dignitaries arriving at the funeral home. Then there were shots of the funeral cortège leaving for the cemetery.

"At the cemetery, only a small group were

allowed to attend the graveside services," the woman announcer said.

As the camera panned to the group around the grave, Donna pushed her plate of food aside.

"That's it!" she said, leaning forward toward the screen.

"That's what?" Abbey said.

"David Gould — he did hand something to Hazelkorn! I knew it! It was sneaky, but I saw it."

"Calm down," Abbey said. "We're also looking for the Woman in Black, remember? We haven't seen even one shot of her yet."

Donna settled back. "That's true, Abbey. We saw them taking pictures at the cemetery. Why don't any shots show the taxicab?"

"Well, it's all over now," Abbey said. "They've gone on to the next story." Absentmindedly, she picked up an eggroll and bit into it. Despite her emotional distress, Abbey's hearty appetite was returning.

"Listen, Abbey. I wish I could see any *extra* videotape that was shot today," Donna said.

"I get it." Abbey picked up the phone. "You want me to call Mr. Hazelkorn and ask if he can get someone to run it for you?"

Donna nodded. "Tell him we'd like to see it as soon as possible, Abbey. I have an awful feeling there's no time to waste. Someone else could get hurt."

The big electric clock at Studio 13 registered 9:30 when Donna and Abbey were let into the theater through the stage door.

"It's so nice of you to do this for us, Mr. Hazelkorn," Donna told the producer.

"It's no problem," Abe Hazelkorn told her, leading the two girls down a hallway to a small screening room. "I'm co-producer of 'The Teenage Talent Show' and the 'Six O'Clock News,' so I have easy access to both."

The producer's face was drawn and tired; it was obvious he was still hurting from the shock of his star's death. With an effort, he said, "You understand that we shoot maybe thirty, forty minutes of material in order to get the three or four minutes we finally put on camera for the show. Any material we don't use is called an 'outtake.' "

"I see," Donna said.

In the screening room, Mr. Hazelkorn picked up a tape and inserted it into a projection machine. "Now you'll see that they've cut out the biggest part of what they shot today, both at the funeral home and the cemetery."

"Where's the extra film now?" Donna asked. "I mean, the outtakes?"

"They discarded about thirty minutes' action," Mr. Hazelkorn said. "It's already gone into disposal. If we tried to save extra film, we'd need a warehouse a mile long." He started the machine. "What I'm going to show you now is about eight minutes of film they ran just before they cut it down to the four minutes that were used on the news."

Donna hid her disappointment about the missing film as she watched the news open with footage of Rick's casket being taken out of the funeral home. Then it switched to shots of limousines arriving at the cemetery and then over to the ceremony.

"There isn't anything showing the taxi or the Woman in Black," Abbey whispered to Donna.

"Right," Donna said, focusing on the flickering screen. Nothing interesting. Nothing . . . until suddenly she saw something.

"Please, Mr. Hazelkorn! Can you stop here and run that last thirty seconds over again?" Donna asked.

"Absolutely." He pushed a button and stopped the tape. "Want me to run it in slow motion?"

Donna shook her head. "No, thanks." She wasn't about to let the producer see exactly what she was looking for.

The film ran again and this time Donna noticed it in detail. As the minister was delivering the speech eulogizing the late star, somewhere in the crowd, behind him, a hand took something black and put it into the pocket of a green oilskin coat. Then she *was* right — David Gould *had* passed something to someone. And that green oilskin coat was Abe Hazelkorn's!

She said nothing as the film clip ran to the end.

"Got what you were looking for?" Mr. Hazelkorn said.

"It was a help," Donna answered. "I really appreciate it, Mr. Hazelkorn."

Two minutes later they were back in the car and heading toward the center of town.

"I saw it." Abbey said. "Very plainly."

"Did Mr. Hazelkorn notice?"

"He absolutely did not," Abbey said smugly.

"How do you know?"

"Because I accidentally on purpose dropped my pocketbook just before the film was rolling that scene. He looked down and picked it up for me."

Donna grabbed her sister and hugged her. "That was brilliant, Abbey."

"Then why are you being so basically depressed again?"

"The woman in the taxi. I can't help feeling she's important." Donna sighed. "But if they threw away the tape, I guess that's that."

"Stop!" Abbey yelled. "There's Hagelmeyer's. Apple strudel and coffee! That'll do it."

"Now you're talking, Abbey." Donna smiled as she pulled the car into the parking lot beside the restaurant. "I need time to think."

"I need strudel," Abbey said. "With globs of whipped cream on top."

Inside the friendly, old-fashioned German coffee shop, right near the college campus, Abbey quickly finished her portion and looked up from her plate. "How about another piece, Donna?"

"Are you sure you want it? There's five hundred calories in that apple strudel — without the whipped cream."

"I guess I'll pass it up," Abbey said. "It's a shame."

At that moment, Donna noticed a young boy carrying a stack of newspapers for sale. She said, "The paper! I forgot the newspapers!" She called the newsboy over and handed him some change.

"An *Evening Express*, please," she said, eagerly taking a copy.

She turned the pages quickly. "There must be some pictures of the funeral here."

Abbey peered over her shoulder until Donna stopped at a full-page story about

Rick Roberts. There were several pictures, some of the funeral.

"Uh-uh," said Abbey, "*nada*. Nothing."

"Right," Donna said. "No taxi. No woman, either."

"Stymied again," Abbey said.

"No, wait!" Donna said. "They throw away tape they don't use at the TV studio. They must do the same thing with pictures at the newspaper. Right?"

"Right!" Abbey said. "Listen, Donna, I know a boy who works at the *Express*."

"You do?" Donna said.

"Scott Brown, a photography intern there." Abbey grinned. "He's crazy about me. Maybe he's there now."

"Here." Donna pushed a coin across the table. "Go call him — please."

Five minutes later, Abbey was back, smiling broadly.

"Is he going to do it?" Donna asked.

"Of course he is," Abbey said, flinging back her head. "I told you, the boy's mad for me."

Ten minutes later Donna and Abbey were in the busy city room of the *Evening Express*, where a slim young man was waiting for them. He was poised and confident as Abbey introduced him to her sister.

"I've heard of you, Miss Rockford," he said. "When Abbey told me what she wanted, I dashed to the files and grabbed every shot of the funeral I could find. I'll show them to you, if you'll follow me."

"I appreciate this, Scott," Donna said as she and Abbey trailed him through the busy room to a small, beat-up desk in a corner.

"Here you are, Miss Rockford." Scott indicated a pile of photographs.

Donna looked at him gratefully. "This is wonderful of you, Scott." She took his hand and shook it. "And please call me Donna."

The young man smiled, just as a raucous voice rasped its way across the room.

"Scott!" The three looked up to see an angry editor pounding his desk and glaring in their direction.

"Excuse me," Scott said. "Duty calls." He walked down the aisle toward the waiting editor.

"He's cool, isn't he?" Abbey said.

"Yes," Donna said, thinking, maybe a little too cool. She looked down at the photographs that had been taken that very morning at Rick Roberts' funeral. "What have we here? Hmmm. . . ." She handed half the pile to Abbey. "Here, you look through these. Anything with the woman or the taxi is what we want."

"Got it," Abbey said, starting to leaf through the pictures.

A minute later, Abbey held up a photo. "This one! It's got the taxi and the woman getting out of it."

Donna took it from her. "Nice going, Abbey. I've got another one of her standing alone."

Abbey looked at it. "But she's so small in these pictures. It's hard to make out much of anything about her."

"Especially with that veil she's wearing," Donna said.

"Well, let's take these. Scott said we could have them," Abbey said.

A minute later, she and Donna headed out of the bustling office. "So long, Scott!" Abbey called out as they were leaving. "Thanks a lot!"

They got back in the car and Donna started to drive toward her apartment.

"Not yet," Abbey said. "Drive me to the house first."

"Why?" Donna asked.

"You'll see," said Abbey. "Don't be so nosy."

As Donna pulled up outside the Rockford family home, Abbey said, "Be right back," and scrambled out of the car. Two minutes later, she came running down the front steps.

"Let's go!" She slammed into the front seat. "And don't ask questions. It's *my* turn to keep a secret."

When they got back to Donna's apartment, Abbey made some hot chocolate while Donna set up the photos on the desk beside her reading lamp.

"Okay," Donna said when Abbey came over carrying two steaming cups of hot chocolate. "They're all yours. Tell me what you see."

"Not without this," Abbey said. She took a large magnifying glass out of her purse. "It's superstrength. That's why I stopped at the house."

"Where'd you get it?" Donna asked.

"I bought it — for my pores," Abbey said. "You wouldn't know about that, the way you abuse your complexion."

"No lectures, please," Donna said. "But it was smart thinking. Now, the pictures. . . ."

Abbey held the strong magnifying glass over the photo of the woman standing on the edge of the grass. "Well, I'll tell you one thing right away," she said. "She's not young."

"How can you tell?"

"Look at her clothes. They're not the kind any young woman would wear. Why, my deah," Abbey continued in her best English accent, "I positively wouldn't be caught dead in them."

"Give me a break," Donna said. "What else do you see?"

"She's poor. Not only are her shoes not very stylish, but look at her purse. I'll bet it's a cheap imitation leather, and it looks worn in places, too."

"Tell me more," Donna said.

Abbey took up another photo of the woman getting out of the taxi. "She's definitely more than middle-aged. Look how bent over she is. Poor thing probably has arthritis or something like that."

"Everyone bends over getting out of a cab." Donna stopped.

"The taxi!"

"What about the taxi?"

"Give me that glass!" Donna took it and held it over the picture closely. "Hmm . . . this printing on the door: LIBERTY RADIO CAB . . . 555-0900. Then there's the number 38."

"I get it," Abbey said. "But what's the 38?"

"Probably the number of the cab." Donna sounded hopeful now. "I'll phone Mario and tell him our next step."

"Which is?" Abbey said.

"Tomorrow morning, we're visiting the Liberty Radio Cab Company."

It was bitter cold the next day as Mario drove Donna and Abbey through icy streets to the dingy wooden shack that served as the office of the Liberty Radio Cab Company.

As they came through the door, the head dispatcher sat behind a scarred wooden desk chewing on a cheap cigar. "You folks need a cab?" he asked.

"We need information," Mario said, flashing his badge. "We're trying to track down a woman who took one of your cabs to Whispering Knoll Cemetery yesterday around ten-thirty."

"You know the number of the cab?" the dispatcher said.

"Thirty-eight," Abbey said.

"Thirty-eight. Hmm . . . that's Al," the dispatcher said. "You're in luck. He hasn't gone out yet."

He looked over toward a group of men warming themselves beside a kerosene heater and called to a balding man. "Al, you take a woman out to Whispering Knoll yesterday morning?"

The man got up and came over to them. "Sure," he said. "Nice lady, all dressed in black. I picked her up at the Ascot Hotel, corner of Vermont and Franklin."

"Do you know her name?" Donna asked.

"Not me. I just took the call," the cabbie replied.

"There's no name here," the dispatcher said, checking a printed pad. "It just says: 'Woman . . . lobby . . . Ascot Hotel.' That's it."

"Did she say anything during the trip?" Donna asked the taxi driver. "Anything at all?"

"She didn't say one word the whole trip. I took her to the cemetery, she got out for a few minutes, then got back in and I drove her to the Ascot Hotel again."

"Okay, thanks," Mario said.

A few minutes later, after a drive that led them to a neglected section of the city, the detective's car pulled up outside the Ascot Hotel. It was a small, soot-covered, gray brick building. A broken neon sign proclaimed: H TEL A COT.

"Whatta dump!" Abbey said in a Bette

Davis tone. Then she added sympathetically, "I told you she was poor."

"It's not exactly the Stanton Savoy," Donna said. "I feel sorry for her."

The carpeting in the lobby was soiled and worn. An ancient, dented coffee machine stood in one corner, while a dusty chandelier hung crookedly from the ceiling.

A tired-looking, white-haired clerk came up behind the tiny front desk as they approached.

Detective Garcia showed his badge and said, "Do you have a guest in this hotel — an older woman who was picked up in the lobby by a cab yesterday morning?"

The clerk scratched his head and thought the question over silently.

"Here." Mario Garcia showed him a police blowup of the photo from the *Evening Express*. "She was all dressed in black."

"Oh, sure." The clerk had obviously decided to talk. "Lady in number twenty-two. She's gone now — checked out yesterday. Her name's here." He turned the register book around toward them. "See it there? . . . 'Strober . . . Mrs. Diana Strober.' "

Donna made note of the name and the address beside it: 210 Charles Street, New York City.

"New York City," Donna said. "It's another reason for us to go up there tomorrow."

"Why not today?" Abbey said. "No, don't tell me. If we study today, and maybe into the night, we can finish and be ready for our exams next week."

"What's wrong with that?"

"Nothing — as long as we get there tomorrow. I can't wait," Abbey said.

A blast of cold air greeted them as they left the hotel. As Donna shivered, the young detective asked, "How about a ride home?"

"Mario, I'd love it," Donna said. "I'm really tired."

"Yes, Mario, let's give the old woman a lift," Abbey said. "She's cracking up. Her age, you know."

"You weren't looking so fabulous yourself," Mario said, opening the door of his car for the two sisters. "I mean, back at the studio a few days ago."

"Really, Mario, sometimes you can be very uncouth," Abbey said.

Donna and Mario exchanged looks. Abbey was obviously recovering, with her customary bounce, from the shock of Rick Roberts' untimely death.

"He's got it bad for you," Abbey said, after Mario bid them good-bye at their house.

"Abbey, please," Donna said. Privately she was worried, remembering Pete's ultimatum to her. But she couldn't dwell on it — she had plenty of other things to think about.

Three things, above all, bothered her most. Who was Diana Strober? Where was Johnny Argyle, and why had he left in such a secret way? And the really most annoying thing was a tiny object — that little three-inch piece of pink plastic. What was it — and what did it mean to Johnny Argyle?

"This room is a mess," Abbey said, looking around in disgust. She looked over at her sister, who was in deep thought in the bay window, cracking peanut shells, but not eating the nuts.

It was eight o'clock at night and cold and dark outside Donna's apartment.

"Did you hear what I said? Come out of your trance. This place is a wreck!" Abbey indicated the remains of their meal, the newspapers lying about, the crumpled Kleenex and other oddments. "It should be condemned by the Board of Health." She stopped. "*Yoo hoo!* Can you hear me?"

Her sister looked up. "Were you speaking to me?"

"No, I was reciting the Gettysburg Address." Abbey threw an arm dramatically in an arc. "Look at this! What do you want me to do with all this garbage?" She sniffed. "I can tell you won't be much help."

"You gave yourself the answer." Donna ran a hand through her tangled hair. "Please be an angel, Abbey. Pick up the trash, dump it in a sack, and take it out, please?"

"I don't mind," Abbey said. "Where do you leave it — out in the hall?"

"No, new rules. Everyone has to carry her junk out to the alleyway downstairs." Donna paused. "Want me to go with you?"

Abbey, already filling the big black plastic

bag with assorted papers, shook her head. "Never mind. I can see you're doing some heavy thinking. Look, Ma, I'll do it myself." The bag was practically bursting now with its contents.

Abbey reached for a rubber band, closed the bag at the top, slung it over her shoulder, opened the door, and was singing, "*Yo ho, yo ho! It's off to work we go . . .*" as she started downstairs.

Donna smiled, then picked up a note pad and started writing quickly. She headed the paper MOTIVE; then left three lines and wrote SUSPECTS. In a moment, she was deep in thought again.

Abbey reached the bottom of the steps, then walked down the back hall to the rear entrance. She was still humming the *Snow White* melody when she opened the door and stepped down to the courtyard. As she headed for the pile of trash bags at the end of the alley, she did not see the dark figure that stepped out from behind the building until it was too late. In a moment, she was under attack.

An arm seized her from behind and held her tight. She let out one yelp, but it was choked off by a gloved hand over her mouth. She dropped the bag and kicked back at her assailant, but she could not get a good foothold on the icy pavement. Her attacker held her two arms behind her, so that Abbey was forced to arch her back painfully just to keep her balance. Suddenly, the helplessness of her situation overcame her; she was paralyzed with fright as the stranger moved her backward toward Abbey knew not what. She felt herself beginning to black out as her legs went rubbery beneath her.

Upstairs in the bay window, Donna stopped writing. For some reason, her mind had suddenly gone blank. *What's the matter with me?* she wondered. She decided that she had probably been pushing herself too hard. It wasn't often that her train of thought broke off as abruptly as this. She rubbed her forehead. Then she got up and looked around the room. She smiled. Abbey had done a darned good job. But then, that was Abbey — she could be careless and sloppy, and then she could be terrific. She smiled, thinking of her sister with love. Deep love. And then she felt it. A tingle along her nerve ends. A familiar tingle. A fire flash of fear.

"Oh, no!" she yelled. Flinging open the door she sped down the stairs. She pounded down the hallway to the back door and hurled herself into the courtyard at top speed, until she reached the dead end of the alley. What she saw there froze her in her steps. What looked like her sister Abbey was slumped against the rear wall with someone, some thing, standing menacingly in front of her.

"Abbey!" she screamed.

As Donna lunged toward her sister, there

came the baying of a dog from the yard next door. Before Donna could make another move, a huge brown-and-white body plunged toward her, blocking her path.

It was the big, friendly Saint Bernard from next door. He took one look at the scene and decided it was playtime. He jumped up on Donna, all 185 pounds of him, placed his paws on her shoulders, and started to lick her face.

It was just the break the mysterious attacker needed. Instantly releasing Abbey, who sank to the ground, the intruder crashed through the bushes into the neighboring yard.

"*Romeo!* Get down! Let me go!" Donna pleaded. But the huge, friendly animal was not to be deterred. Donna tried to push him away, using every ounce of strength she had, but it was useless. Romeo was demonstrating his affection; it was all a wonderful game.

Donna, frustrated, wrestling with the dog, was surprised to hear a high, hysterical giggle. That is, it started out as a giggle and blossomed into raucous laughter. Looking down, Donna saw that it came from Abbey.

"I — I can't help it," Abbey wailed between chokes of laughter. "You looked so funny with Romeo slobbering all over you. What a watchdog! He's a mess."

As she spoke, the dog returned and began to lick Abbey's hand lovingly.

"Are you all right?" Donna asked, helping Abbey brush herself off.

"I'm fine," Abbey insisted.

"Did you see who it was?" Donna asked.

"Nope. He kept me turned away from him. Besides, it's so dark out here." She saw Donna's expression. "Don't worry about me, Donna."

But Donna *was* worried. Had Abbey's assailant been lying in wait in the alley?

Upstairs in bed, Donna thought, *I've got to speed up this investigation — before it's too late.*

"I love New York, I love New York," Abbey was singing softly as the Roadways bus approached the Lincoln Tunnel. Before them was spread the panorama of what most people thought was the most exciting city in the world.

Abbey had been humming the "I Love New York" ditty on and off during the hour-and-a-half bus ride from Philadelphia. Now she broke off as she noticed Donna's expression.

"What's the matter? You're so serious."

"I know," Donna said. "I keep wondering who this Diana Strober is. Somehow that name sounds familiar to me."

"Why are you so uptight?" Abbey said. "We'll find out in just a few more minutes.

We're practically where she lives now."

When they reached 210 Charles Street, they weren't prepared for what they found.

It was a nursing home.

The sign over the entrance read CHARLES STREET HOME FOR THE ELDERLY. The outside of the building had dark tan brick walls and old-fashioned windows and looked old but respectable.

Inside, it was quite another story. The front doors opened into a large lobby that was filled with many old and feeble people. Some were in wheelchairs, some hobbled on canes or crutches, some simply sat on the dilapidated sofas and chairs.

All the patients had a look of resigned desperation, and who could blame them? The walls were a sickly green, peeling and patched over by crude attempts at plastering. A black-and-white television set that had seen much better days gave off fuzzy images that intermittently vanished completely from the screen. Neither Abbey nor Donna had ever seen people in such a state of hopelessness and misery, although with a mother who was a doctor, they had been in quite a few hospitals and sanitoriums.

"Isn't it pitiful?" Abbey whispered to Donna, her eyes wide with compassion.

Before Donna could answer, a woman in a white nurse's uniform came up to them.

"May I help you?" she asked politely enough.

She was a woman of about sixty, full

bosomed and imposing in stature. She had dark hair with a streak of white running from her forehead to a bun that she wore coiled around the top of her head. All in all, she had a severe but kind face. If looks meant anything, Donna thought, this woman was an efficient, perhaps stern, but surely compassionate administrator — if that's who she was. Donna's guess proved to be correct.

"I'm Mrs. Yglesias," the woman said. "And you? . . ."

"I'm Donna Rockford," Donna said. "And this is my sister, Abbey. We're from Philadelphia."

The woman surveyed them quickly, then said, "Won't you come into my office?"

They followed her into a small, dingy but clean office, with a desk, a few chairs, and some files against the wall. On the desk was a sign: SABINA YGLESIAS, DIRECTOR.

Without waiting, Donna explained why they had come there.

"Diana Strober?" The director's face softened. "Yes, she works here. I hope there's no trouble."

It's funny she should think that, Donna thought. Aloud, she said, "Oh, no, nothing like that."

"I'm glad," Mrs. Yglesias said, relieved. "She's a very fine woman. I wouldn't want her to have any more problems. . . ." She caught herself. "I shouldn't have said that. We all have our troubles." She stopped and looked at Donna with inquiring eyes.

"I would just like to have a few words with her," Donna said.

"You've come all the way from Philadelphia just to speak to her?" The woman sounded skeptical.

Making a quick decision, Donna took her wallet out of her purse and flicked it open to her police identification card, with her picture and the signature of the police chief in Philadelphia.

"Why, I read something about you in the newspaper not too long ago," Mrs. Yglesias said approvingly.

"You must mean the article in the *Times*," Abbey burst in eagerly. "About the man they found in the Lincoln Memorial in Washington. Donna solved that crime."

Donna was for once glad of Abbey's loquaciousness. She was rapidly thinking that she preferred not to mention Rick Roberts in any way, which meant she had to come up with some likely story.

"I'm not here on behalf of the police," she said, and saw the director relax. "The basic reason that I'm here" — she frantically tried to think of something that would not be an outright lie — "is that there are some people who are interested in Mrs. Strober. Nothing that could in any way be harmful to her. It's more or less a case of their wanting to know a little about her background, that's all."

The director knitted her brows. "Well, there I can't help you," she said almost apologetically. "She came to work here about a year ago. Because we gave her a room here and her meals, she said she wouldn't expect much in the way of salary. She's quiet, minds her own business, and she's wonderful to our residents. They truly love her. However, Mrs. Strober has gone away for a few days. I can call you when she returns."

At that moment, a male attendant came to the glass partition separating the office from the lobby and rapped on the window. "We need you," he mouthed through the glass.

Mrs. Yglesias instantly jumped up. "Please excuse me. It's an emergency." She hurried toward the door.

When the door opened, the girls heard the attendant. ". . . really very upset, crying . . . he's very depressed." The two left quickly.

"Who wouldn't be depressed in a hideous place like this?" Abbey said indignantly. "Boy, if this is a city-run home, there must be something wrong with the city."

Donna cut her off sharply. "Hush, Abbey. I've got something I want you to do. Only you can do it."

Abbey's eyes lit up. "Great — what is it?"

"I want to get a look at Diana Strober's room. Think you can manage it?"

"Of course I can. I need a minute, to think." She pressed her hand to her temples.

"What are you trying to do?" Donna asked. "Squeeze it out of your brain?"

"Please, I must concentrate." Abbey flashed indignant dark brown eyes at her sister, then went back into her trance.

In a few minutes, Mrs. Yglesias came back, all apologies. "Nothing serious, thank heaven," she said. "Poor Mr. Contini, he suffers from chronic depression. But we gave him his medication. He'll be all right."

"This is a very big place, isn't it?" Abbey asked.

"We have two hundred residents — most of them two in a room."

"Well, where does Mrs. Strober live? Does she have her own room?" Abbey asked innocently.

"Yes, but it's a very small one, I'm afraid," the director said. "Why do you ask?"

Abbey gulped and took the big leap. "Well, our mother is a doctor, you know? You probably read about it in the *Times* article." The director nodded. "Mother says that it's good for the patients when the people who work in a hospital, or someplace like that, live right there. Do you agree?"

Mrs. Yglesias nodded vigorously. "Oh, I do, I do. It gives the residents a sense of security; they don't feel abandoned to strangers at night." She met Abbey's intense brown eyes and succumbed, as so many had before her.

"Would you like to see my room? And Diana's? The residents are always free to visit us there."

"It would be wonderful," Abbey said enthusiastically. "Then we could tell our mother how your system works here."

Five minutes later, the director was showing them through dingy corridors upstairs.

"The live-in porters and kitchen help have these rooms on the left," she said. "And that one is Diana's. Mine is this one. . . ."

The girls looked through the open door into a neat — if starkly unattractive — room. While Abbey kept Mrs. Yglesias busy with her chatter — a talent that never failed her — Donna peeked into the adjoining room.

Mrs. Strober's room was even more stark, more impersonal, than the director's. From the doorway, Donna could see a narrow bed, a chest of drawers, a small rocker, and a costume trunk, the old-fashioned kind used by theater troupers in the early half of the century. On the trunk, a Spanish shawl was draped neatly. On top of that was a pile of magazines and a small oval picture of a family group.

The trunk was only a few feet from the doorway; Donna decided to risk it. She quickly stepped into the room and looked through the small pile of magazines. But most of them were not magazines at all. They were puzzle books: crossword puzzles, anagrams, word games. A closer glance at the family picture revealed a man, woman, and child — all too small for Donna to make anything of in her haste.

Hearing Abbey's voice suddenly rise to a higher pitch — a warning signal between them — Donna hurried to Mrs. Yglesias' room in time to pick up another little morsel of Abbey's invention. ". . . because when I was little and had my tonsils out, I remember wanting my family with me in the hospital. I made such a fuss, they let everyone stay — my mother, father, sister." Pause. "They wouldn't let my dog in, though."

Seeing Donna, Mrs. Yglesias said, "If there's anything else I can tell you. . . ."

Donna said, "Did Mrs. Strober say where she was going? How long she would be away?"

"She mentioned something about New Hampshire. Pinkney, I believe. She had to see a lawyer." Mrs. Yglesias frowned. "And she said she'd be back by Friday."

"Does she travel like that very often?" Donna said.

"Not much. She was away yesterday and the day before. I don't know where she went, but she just took a little overnight bag." The director smiled ruefully. "Come to think of it, these two trips are the first she's taken since she came here last year."

Donna said, "You've been very helpful. I only wish we could do something to help you." She indicated the shabby lobby, the dispirited people.

"We need so much here, I don't know where we'd begin. Diana is very upset about it, too. Still, even a little money spent properly could make a big difference."

She saw the two girls to the outside

entrance and waved as they went down the steps. "I'll let you know when she comes back."

In the street, Abbey asked, "What's up? What did you get?"

"Not much." Donna bit her lip. "Something bothers me about that Strober woman."

"I'm starving," Abbey said. "What's our next move? The High School of Theater Arts?"

"You've got it," Donna said. "Come on."

The High School of Theater Arts was an old, faded-red building that had been built in the early 1900's. It looked out of place on Fifty-third Street, with all the towering, modern steel and glass skyscrapers surrounding it.

"Donna, stop me, I'm fainting," Abbey said. "Just take one look at *that!*"

Donna looked. The street was like a stage. On the sidewalk, several students in varying states of dress were doing their thing. Some were practicing dance steps, others were reciting bits of speeches from plays, still others were singing as if to an audience.

"Nothing to get excited about," Donna said. "They're theater students. They're just doing their homework."

"They look like they're having such fun," Abbey said wistfully as she and Donna went up the few broad stone steps leading into this unusual high school.

Inside, at an information desk, a police

guard stopped them. When they told him what they wanted, the guard said, "Ask her. She knows everything." He indicated an office marked VIVIAN MOSS, PH.D., and under it the title PRINCIPAL.

They got action in the principal's office. Dr. Moss, a handsome woman in her fifties, stylishly dressed, responded instantly to Donna's question.

"Rick Roberts? I certainly do remember him. He's one of our most famous alumni." She stopped herself. "Or I should say he *was* one of our most famous students."

"That's right, Dr. Moss," Donna said. "I guess the whole country knows about his tragic accident."

Dr. Moss said, "He was a lovely young man. Bright, polite, a model student in every way. What a pity he had to die so young." She sighed. "What is it that you want? Information about Rick? We have his school records."

Donna said, "Actually I wanted to see his class yearbook — nineteen seventy-two, I think."

"I don't see why not," the principal said. "It's public information. Wait right here." She hurried out of the office and returned a few minutes later holding a green leather volume.

"Here you are," she said brightly. "Draw up your chairs and take your time. I have my work to do, so feel comfortable."

Donna could hardly wait to get her hands on the book. She quickly thumbed the pages until they came to the R's and there it was, a picture of the young Rick Roberts, eighteen years old.

"Wasn't he a knockout?" Abbey said.

He was handsome, Donna thought. But then she read the print under his picture. It was only four or five lines: *He thinks he's as great as his father, but he's only half as great — like his profile. Catch the left side sometime.*

Donna and Abbey looked at each other. "I don't see anything so sensational in that, do you?" Abbey said.

"It's interesting," Donna said thoughtfully. She thumbed further through the book. Evidently, Rick Roberts had participated in very few extracurricular activities. The whole thrust of his academic career had been acting.

Dr. Moss confirmed this. "Rick was practically obsessed with the theater. We were all quite surprised when he settled for being the host of a television show." She sighed, remembering. "But that's show business, you know. He made such a name for himself, he became almost as famous as his father."

"Did you know his father?" Donna asked.

"Oh, yes, he came to school several times to see his son perform." She smiled, reminiscing again. "And I remember the night Rick Roberts, Senior, invited the whole class to the theater to see him in *Hamlet*. He was brilliant. What an inspiration for a son."

The school bell sounded and Dr. Moss

jumped up. "I have to go now," she said. "You can stay, if you like."

"Thank you. We've got what we wanted," Donna said.

As they headed for the bus terminal Abbey said, "Did you really get what you wanted?"

"More than I need, Abbey," Donna said.

"Tell me!" Abbey said. "I don't get it at all. Just a couple of dopey remarks in a yearbook. I don't know what Kitty Kenway meant in her column."

"She's a very bright woman," Donna said. "At least she has a deep understanding of human nature."

"Okay, if you're not going to tell me," Abbey said. They were at the terminal now. Abbey reached for a candy bar at the newsstand they were passing. "I'll console myself with a nice chocolate bar. With almonds. I'll get even."

"You'll get pimples," Donna said.

"There's our bus back to Philadelphia," Abbey yelled, and they both ran for it. They made it just in time. Inside the bus they settled back for the ride home.

Neither of them had any idea of what awaited them there.

ELEVEN

From the moment they walked into the house, there was trouble.

"Thank heavens you're back!" their mother, Dr. Rockford, said. "We've been terribly worried about you!"

Their father, after kissing them, said, "Thank God, you're here safe." He led them to the dining room, where a hot meal was set out on the buffet sideboard.

"I don't get it," Donna said. "Why are you both so agitated?"

"We've plenty of reason to be," her father said.

"Help yourself to some food, and we'll explain," her mother said.

It was bewildering. The girls hadn't the faintest idea of what it could be.

"How was the trip to New York?" her father said. "Anything unusual happen?"

"Nothing at all," Donna said. "Do you want to hear about it?"

"We certainly do," her mother said. "And don't leave anything out."

Donna returned to the table with a platter filled with roast beef and mashed potatoes and gravy, while in her other hand she held a small bowl of tossed salad.

"All right, I'll tell you," she began and gave her parents a detailed account of the day in New York City. When she had finished, her father put down his knife and fork.

"What I am going to say is extremely important, Donna. Listen very carefully."

This in itself was most unusual. It was not the practice in the Rockford home to have serious discussions at meal time. Dr. Rockford insisted that people not bring their problems to the dinner table; she said it was neither good for their health nor for the family relationship.

But now both parents were deadly serious.

"We are going to ask you, Donna, to take yourself off the Roberts case," her father said.

"What?" Donna said. "I can't believe you're asking that, Dad."

She had a right to say that.

Long ago the Rockfords had agreed that Donna could pursue a career in criminal investigation; they were deeply interested in her criminal psychology classes at the university.

"This case is different from any other," her father said. "We've never received anything like this!"

He reached into his inner jacket pocket and took out a long envelope.

"Whoever wrote that letter means business," Dr. Rockford said. "Let her read it, George."

Donna took the letter. What met her eyes was a message that was a hodgepodge of printed letters of the alphabet obviously clipped from newspapers and magazines. The individual letters looked ludicrous, but the message they spelled out was terrifying:

GET YOUR DAUGHTER OFF THE CASE
IF YOU WANT HER TO LIVE.

"I see what you mean," Donna said, shaken. She added, "May I see the envelope, Dad?"

Donna studied the envelope carefully. Her parents' names were printed in crudely disguised lettering. There was no return address, only a postmark, PHILADELPHIA, FEB. 10, 1982, and a stamp — a colorful one, with a shamrock and the motto "Erin go bragh." Donna was carefully examining it when her father said, "See why we're upset, Donna?"

"Listen, Dad, Mother — whoever wrote this doesn't know very much about me — or you. Every time I work on a case — *any case* — I'm taking a chance. Every investigator does. This person who's trying to scare us isn't very bright."

Her mother settled back in her chair. "Explain, Donna."

"If somebody wanted to scare you into taking me off the case, why wouldn't he — or she — give you the message by phone? Twelve words. That's all it is. This note looks to me like a childish stunt. Amateurish. I don't think it's a real threat."

"You can't take that chance, Donna," her father said. "While you may be right. . . ."

The doorbell rang. Abbey yelled, "I'll get it!" and streaked toward the door.

The newcomer was Mario Garcia, whom Donna's father welcomed warmly. "Why, Mario, you've picked the right time to come by. Please take a look at this."

Mario greeted the others, then took the letter and envelope and carefully read it.

"What do you make of it?" Mr. Rockford asked him.

Mario said, "I assume this is making waves in the Rockford family?"

"You assume correctly," Dr. Rockford said. "We think this means real danger for Donna. What's your opinion, Mario?"

The young detective hesitated before answering. "We get crank notes all the time at headquarters. Ninety-nine times out of a hundred, they're a hoax," he said. "Still, where there's suspicion of murder. . . ."

"But, Mario," Donna said, "so far, the coroner is treating the case as an accidental death."

"But until we know definitely how Rick

Roberts died, murder *is* a possibility," Mario said. "There is an element of danger here, but this looks phony to me. There are heavy odds this wasn't put together by a killer." He held the note up. "Why go to all this trouble? A phone call would make more sense."

As Donna thanked him with a look, her mother sighed and said, "We knew it would be like this, didn't we, George? I guess we'll have to trust Donna's judgment once again." She seized her daughter's hand. "You will be careful, darling?"

When Donna nodded, Dr. Rockford said, "Your father and I have to leave tonight for a few days. There's a conference in Atlanta, and Grandma Rockford isn't feeling too well. We should be back by Tuesday, at the latest."

Donna said, "Thank you both for your confidence in me. I promise I'll be careful."

Dr. Rockford said, "Why couldn't we have a daughter who wants to be a secretary, a beautician — something harmless like that?"

"Because twenty years ago, when very few women were doing it, you decided to be a doctor," George Rockford said. "I wonder what the next few years will bring? What will Abbey be?"

"An astronaut — just like Sally Ride!" Abbey jumped up from the table. "I'm going to live in a space station and raise my children there. My husband will be a planet jumper. You know, Mars, Jupiter, Pluto. . . ."

When they stopped laughing, the Rockford

parents said their good-byes and left, and Abbey went upstairs.

"Mario, please come into the living room." Donna took his arm. "I have something to ask you."

In the living room, the fire was flickering low. Mario looked at Donna admiringly. In the dark room, her brown hair and hazel eyes picked up the glints of firelight, and her skin was rosy, adding color and vivacity to her own special brand of good looks.

Suddenly, Mario tipped her face up and brought his lips down to hers. She did not protest. For one long moment, it was wonderful being in his arms, knowing that he cared for her, responding to his kiss. In the next moment, she thought of Pete; a wave of guilt swept over her.

"What's the matter?" Mario said huskily. "Is kissing me so terrible?"

Her cheeks blushed crimson, and not from the heat of the fire. "It isn't that, Mario." She stopped, not knowing how to go on. How could she tell him her feelings, her confusion in this moment, knowing that she really cared for Pete O'Brien, and yet could respond to Mario's kiss the way she did? This was not the first time Mario had kissed her, but she felt just as embarrassed, as uncomfortable as she had then. *What's wrong with me?* Donna thought. *How can I like being kissed by anyone but Pete?*

It made her realize more than ever that

she was too immature for a lasting relationship — with Pete or anyone. Too young for real love. The thought made her sad, but it helped clear her feelings.

"What did you want to talk to me about?" Mario asked.

"It wasn't important. I forgot." She yawned. "Good night, Mario."

After Mario left, Donna was damping down the fire, when Abbey came into the room.

"You know, you hurt his feelings," she said.

"Oh, no! I thought you were upstairs. How could you do that?" Donna said indignantly.

"It was easy." Abbey held up a small pair of opera glasses. "I hated having to use these, but it was so dark down here."

"Abbey, you're hopeless," Donna said.

"You look tired," Abbey said. "How about we go upstairs now and fall apart?"

"I sure can use it," Donna said, heading for the stairs. "This case is driving me berserk. Can we talk?"

"You bet," Abbey said, walking into the guest room with her sister. It was a golden room with sunny yellow carpeting and Oriental bamboo furniture. There was a huge double bed and a twin-size one matching it, both with furry white-and-gold bedspreads, heaped with soft cushions in all shades. Tonight, it was a glorious, restful haven for Donna and Abbey.

"If it was no accident," Donna said, "I want to tick off the possible suspects."

"Tick away," Abbey said. She was slipping into a lovely white silk nightgown and robe that their mother had laid out. There was one set for Donna also.

"Let's start at the top and work down. Abe Hazelkorn, the producer. Maybe he hated such a temperamental star as Rick. As a matter of fact, the same thing applies to David Gould, the audio man; to Monte Clark, the announcer. . . ."

To Donna's surprise, Abbey interrupted with, ". . . to Rex Vicente. . . ." She paused and said, "I admit it, Donna. It looks like Rick Roberts wasn't everything people thought he was."

Donna touched her sister's arm. "I remember reading that one reason Rex Vicente was turned down for the conductor's job at the Lincoln Philharmonic was that Rick Roberts kept calling him 'The Wreck,' which made him a figure to ridicule . . . the wrong image for a symphony orchestra."

"I guess Rick's sense of humor wasn't always so hot," Abbey said unhappily.

"Certainly Howard Reilly had reason to hate Rick. He was getting fired — just as he was about to retire with a full pension."

"Do you think he could've been the one? . . ."

Donna slipped into bed and pulled a silky yellow sheet up around her. "I don't know the man, I haven't seen him. But that also means, Abbey, that his daughter could have been angry enough to want to hurt Rick, too.

Father or daughter? Either one could've done it."

"Or both." Abbey, leaning on an elbow in the bed next to Donna's, batted her long, dark eyelashes. "And don't forget Lana Lawrence. As the poet said, 'Hell hath no fury.' "

"The actual quote is, *'Heaven has no rage like love to hatred turned/ Nor Hell a fury like a woman scorned.'* And the poet was William Congreve, in his play *The Mourning Bride.*"

"You're too smart, Donna. It gets boring."

"Be serious. You were right about Lana. She certainly must've resented Rick terribly. He almost ruined her career — and her life." Then Donna added, unhappily, "I hate to say this, but when it comes to suspects, last and absolutely not least is the gofer — Johnny Argyle."

"But what reason would he have?" Abbey asked. "Remember, Bonnie told us Johnny adored Rick."

"Feelings change, Abbey. From the little I overheard, Rick was in a rotten mood that day."

"What I can't understand," Abbey said, filing the tip of a long, pale pink fingernail, "is exactly what the accident was. I mean, I know the rope slipped and the parallel bars fell." She looked up, her big, almost black eyes gleaming. "But why did they land right on top of poor Rick?"

"That's a good question. We'll try to find out by . . ." Donna began, when they heard a loud crash from downstairs and then a thud.

"What was that?" Abbey said, her face white.

Donna was swinging her feet over the side of the bed and pushing them into her slippers. She grabbed a robe and said in an undertone, "Quiet, Abbey. I'm going down to see what that was!"

"Don't leave me," Abbey wailed. "Wait for me! I'll h-help!" Her teeth were chattering with fear as she tiptoed down the stairs in the dark behind her sister.

TWELVE

There was a faint rustle as Donna went a last step down into the front hallway. It seemed to come from the living room. No longer able to stand the suspense, Abbey, directly behind her sister, called out in a quavery voice, "Who's there?"

There was no answer.

"Let's have a look," Donna said, picking up a small but heavy bronze statue of a dancer from the front entrance table. Together they entered the living room.

There was no one there.

A breeze was blowing from a window, and that was strange, until they looked more closely. The window was broken.

"Look out," Donna said, pointing to the shattered glass on the rug.

"What's that?" Abbey said, pointing to something white that lay in front of the fireplace. She walked across to the fireplace and picked up a heavy gray rock with a note tied to it.

"Another note?" Donna said, taking off the piece of paper. "It looks like we've got a regular pen pal."

"What does it say?" Abbey said. "Let me see."

Both girls read the words, boldly printed in heavy, dark-penciled letters: GIVE UP THE CASE OR DIE!

"Ooh, that's awful," Abbey said.

"Not really," Donna said.

"Are you crazy?" Abbey was trembling. "Look — it says we're going to get killed or something."

"Or nothing. Now this really is getting ridiculous." Donna looked at her sister. "Want to know why? Because the first note took a lot of time to paste up and send through the mail. But now, Mother and Dad leave the house by car with their luggage and we go upstairs to sleep — and what we get a half hour later is this dopey note flung through a window." She shook her head. "It's nothing to shiver over, Abbey."

Abbey started to relax. "I don't see why you think that. Dying isn't funny, Donna — at least from everything I've heard."

"Use your head, Abbey, please. Someone knows we're here, someone sees everyone leave, including Mario and both our parents.

If that person really wants to get us — me, because I'm investigating a case, and you, because you've been working with me —" Donna broke off. "It doesn't make any sense. All this person —" she held up the note — ". . . all this *kook* has to do is ring the doorbell, and when we open the door. . . ."

"*Bang!*" Abbey made her thumb and forefinger into a gun.

"Exactly. Or a dozen things not so crude that would do the trick. Scare us off permanently." Donna grunted. "This guy isn't playing for keeps. And that means that the cops may be wasting their time looking for a murderer." She looked at the broken window and said, "Thank goodness, the folks won't be home tonight. Let's seal up the window and deal with this mess tomorrow."

Abbey was already rummaging at a desk in the corner; she came back with a roll of tape and some sheets of paper. In minutes she had covered the window and they were back upstairs in the bedroom.

"I'm dead for sleep," Abbey said, shucking off her robe. She picked up a small gold perfume atomizer from the vanity table and gently sprayed a cloud of scent on her long, wavy black hair.

"What are you doing?" Donna said. "Putting on perfume to go to *sleep*? How decadent can you get?"

Abbey shoved the perfume bottle at her. "It's soothing. Here, try some?"

"It's unnecessary, not particularly healthful, and" — she looked at the label — "expensive."

As Donna read the name on the bottle — *Quest* — she blinked, looked again, and leaped out of bed. She opened her purse and took out the envelope that held Lana Lawrence's discarded tissue.

"I'm so stupid," she said.

"That's what I keep trying to tell you," Abbey said.

Donna grabbed her sister. "We've been so busy running around, chasing people, I forgot about *things*. Tomorrow morning, as soon as we get up, we'll go to the stores and locate Lana's perfume."

"I gave you a lead, didn't I?" Abbey asked. "Always glad to give you a hand, champ."

The two sisters smiled at each other, turned off the lights, got into their big downy beds with the fat, puffed, white-and-gold quilts, and dropped quickly off to sleep.

"It's not any brand *we* sell," the saleswoman said. They were at the perfume counter in Albee's Department Store. "But I'll check further. The buyer will know."

It was 10:00 o'clock the following morning. After a quick breakfast, the two girls had gotten into Donna's red Mustang and driven downtown on the trail of Lana Lawrence's elusive perfume.

That trail was to prove more elusive than they expected.

The buyer at Albee's came over, examined

the crumpled tissue, sniffed, and said, "This isn't one of ours. We can't carry every brand — especially an extraordinarily expensive one like this. If it's as costly as I think it is, it's a brand carried only by world class stores — like Bergdorf Goodman or Saks Fifth Avenue in New York and in Beverly Hills, California. Their customers are the very wealthy or the very famous." She sniffed again. "This is too rich for our blood. Astronomical prices, some of them. Could come to as much as six hundred dollars an ounce."

Donna thanked her and walked out dispiritedly. In the street, Donna sat in the car in silence. For once, Abbey was quiet, watching her sister stare through the windshield.

"Mario! He can help us," Donna said suddenly. She started the car and drove down Chestnut Street, turned right on Ninth, and swung down to the Eighty-eighth Precinct.

"Donna! Abbey!" Mario Garcia came out to the front desk at police headquarters, obviously delighted by the unexpected visit.

He led Donna into his private office, a small, dark, tan-walled cubbyhole with a worn-out brown rug beneath a decrepit wooden desk and mismatched chairs.

"I need a favor, Mario," Donna said. "Can you get in touch with anyone who could do a chemical analysis of perfume?"

"I sure can," Mario said swiftly. "Stuart Rosen. He's your man."

Donna was pleased. "You mean the forensic doctor in the lab? Really?" She pulled out the crumpled envelope with the tissue. "Can you give this to him?"

"I'll do better than that." He smiled. "I'll take you to the lab right now and let you meet him in person."

She could have flung her arms around him in gratitude. But, remembering last night in front of the fireplace, she simply said, "Thanks a lot, Mario. I really appreciate it," and walked quickly out of the little office to Abbey — and safety.

The police lab was divided into sections — *Toxicology, Fingerprints, Ballistics,* and a *Miscellaneous* division.

Detective Garcia, trailed by Donna and Abbey, stopped in front of a door marked CHEMICALS, STUART ROSEN, M.D., PH.D.

A rap on the door brought Dr. Rosen himself. He was a lean, rather handsome man with alert, electric-blue eyes and a deep-tanned face. He had a weary look of having seen too much, known too much — undoubtedly the result of twenty years spent in a lab where so much of his work was intertwined with the sordid reality of crime, of murder. But now, seeing the girls and Detective Garcia, a childish delight lit his face.

"Detective Garcia — this is a pleasure. Come in, come in."

He led the way into a good-sized laboratory, about 15 by 25 feet. It was white-walled, well lit, with a center table laden with analysis equipment running from end to end —

Bunsen burners, tubing endlessly connected to glass tanks, rows of test tubes of various sizes, even a computer hooked up to timers and clocks and gauges in an arrangement incomprehensible to the layman, but obviously a part of Dr. Rosen's own special world.

"Make yourselves comfortable," Dr. Rosen said. They were now in a corner where several stools, a desk, a worktable, and a bulletin board jammed with notes proclaimed this the territory Dr. Rosen had staked out as his own stronghold.

A young man of about 18, in a blue jogging suit, with a friendly face that, although plump, somehow managed to resemble Dr. Rosen's, jumped up from a chair. He dropped the copy of *Physical Culture* magazine he had been reading and managed to overturn the chair, which landed with a bang on the floor, barely missing Abbey's foot.

Bending over to pick up the chair, he looked up and saw Abbey staring down at him. His lower jaw dropped, his eyes bulged, he said, "Oh, sorry," and dropped the chair again.

"Matthew," his father said patiently. "These are friends of Detective Garcia's." To the others, he said, "My son."

Matthew Rosen stood up, banging his head against the shade of a standing lamp beside the desk. To it he said, "Excuse me," then he put his hand out to Abbey and said, "Pleasedtomeetcha," flushing from ear to ear.

Abbey quickly said, "I'm pleased to meet

you, Matthew. Sorry for barging in like this." He blushed a spotted purple.

Dr. Rosen turned to Mario. "What can I do for you?"

"I'll let Miss Rockford explain," he said.

As Donna opened her purse, Dr. Rosen said to his son, "Matthew, you can go now."

Abbey quickly said, "Oh, must he? I thought he could explain some of the laboratory, er, stuff to me."

"It's fine with me," Dr. Rosen said, and smiled as Abbey and his son walked over to the equipment across the room. The doctor whispered, "I hope he doesn't blow up the place. He's my son, and I love him, but I privately think Matthew could be our answer to a nuclear attack. Send him to any foreign country to help them, and they'll self-destruct, I assure you."

When Donna handed Dr. Rosen the crumpled perfumed tissue, he took it lightly between thumb and forefinger, lifted it to his nose, and sniffed. And sniffed again.

"Come with me," he said. He led Donna over to a subdivided area whose wall was covered with 100 or more file cards arranged in alphabetic order. The cards began with ACTION, AFTER DARK, ALONE, APPLE BLOSSOM, and ran all the way through GORGEOUS, HAPPY TIME, and others to end with ZEBRA NO. 2.

"These are the one hundred most popular brands of perfume in America," Dr. Rosen said, "and their chemical breakdown. They've been a great help in some cases." Dr. Rosen sniffed the tissue. "What you've got here, Donna, is a special, customized perfume."

"What does that mean?" Donna asked.

"Chemists these days are concocting their own brands of perfume. Some of them imitate the established scents — say 'Joy,' which sells for about fifty dollars a half ounce. They concoct a reasonable substitute and sell it for half price or less. Others come up with an original perfume and have a very special list of customers — the rich, the famous. They make these perfumes for only a certain clientele and won't sell them to anyone else." He sniffed at the tissue. "I believe that's what this is. I'll need time to check it out."

"How long will it take?" Donna asked.

"Give me a few days. I've got to analyze the formula, then track down the chemists. They're not about to give their secret formulas to anyone, not even the police, unless they have to. But this is a murder case, I presume."

Donna and Dr. Rosen walked back to his office to find Abbey and young Matthew Rosen hunched over the desk, studying a double spread in *Physical Culture*. It showed several musclemen pumping iron, and, as they approached, Matthew stepped back and flexed the bicep of his left arm in an outflung gesture that dislodged a bottle from the shelf behind him. It dropped to the floor and a cloud of caustic vapor rose to their nostrils.

"Sorry, Dad," Matthew said. "I — I dropped the hydrochloric acid. I'll get the mop."

"He's right," Dr. Rosen said, watching his son go. "It *is* hydrochloric acid. If only his physical dexterity matched his mental ability. . . ." He sighed wistfully.

Before Matthew could return, Donna and Abbey said their good-byes and left.

Outside police headquarters, Abbey said, "Now there's a boy I really like. Oh, he's a little clumsy, but. . . ." She looked at her sister. "What's the matter?"

"I can't handle this," Donna said. "Wait for Mrs. Strober, wait for the chemist, wait for poor Mr. Reilly. Everything in this case is *wait*. What we need is *action*!"

"I need *food*," Abbey said. "Hey, we're only a couple of blocks away from Pagano's. How about? . . ."

"You've got it," Donna said. "I'm stumped."

They walked down the busy street to Pagano's, which was crammed with college students, high school kids, shoppers, tourists, visiting families, teachers, and professors.

Behind their car in the parking lot, someone stepped between two cars, crossed quickly to Donna's red Mustang, looked around hastily, then bent down over the rear tire, as if inspecting it. In one hand, the mysterious stranger held something that gleamed in the heavy gray daylight.

Inside Pagano's, Abbey led the way to a big booth in the center of the room. But before she and Donna were seated, a masculine voice said, "Mind if I join you?"

The newcomer was Pete O'Brien. Without waiting for an answer, he slid into Donna's end of the booth, right beside her. From the opposite end, Abbey burst into a wide grin.

"Sit down, Pe-tah," she said, lapsing into her Bette Davis act. "It's so delightful to see you here."

In the next instant, the waiter appeared. "What'll it be?" he asked.

"I'll have a Pagano's One-Hundred-Thousand-Dollar-Prize Pizza," Abbey said in her normal Abbey voice. Then she turned to Peter and dropped into the Davis voice again. "What brought you to this part of town, deah boy?"

"I'll deah boy you," Peter said, pushing a plate of pickles and sour tomatoes at her. "Here, fill your face while I have a serious word with your sister."

Abbey, injured, picked up a pickle and bit thoughtfully into it. "Too sour," she said. "Like you, Pete."

He reached into his pocket and took out some quarters. "Have yourself a crack at Pac-Man or feed the jukebox. And don't come back till your pizza is here."

As Abbey, pouting but secretly pleased, left the table, Donna said, "What's wrong, Pete? And can't it wait?"

"It can't." Pete's face, usually so pleasant and agreeable, was drawn in stern lines. His eyes were hostile and he kept them unrelentingly on Donna. "I'm fed up, Donna. I really am."

"What's this all about?" Donna asked. Her heart started thumping quickly.

"As if you didn't know," Pete said, his tone so sarcastic she barely recognized it as Pete's own. She sat silently as he continued. "It's about you and me." His eyes clouded. "And Mario Garcia. I told you the other night that I was getting sick of waiting. You've got to make your mind up, Donna. I'm not kidding."

Donna looked into what had suddenly become the face of a stranger. She saw only bitterness there and anger. "This isn't the best time in the world to bring up the subject, Pete. I'm actually distraught over this case."

"Well, I'm distraught, too. I don't mind hanging around, Donna" — his voice broke, but he gulped and went on — "because you know how — how I feel about you." He looked up, saw Abbey approaching, and waved her back. She made a face and returned to the jukebox. He said to Donna, "Like I said, I don't mind — much. But when you start paying attention to the Great Detective just because he's always coming on to you. . . ."

"Now stop that," Donna said, angrily. "There isn't a word of truth in what you're saying. It's just — I hate to say this, Pete — jealousy, dumb jealousy."

"Maybe it is, but I don't care. Why, you're with him more than with me. I've had it."

"I'm working on the same case as he is," Donna said impatiently. "All I eat, drink, think, *dream* these days is how to get a handle on the Rick Roberts case. What I don't need is you hassling me." She reached out and touched his arm. "You've never been like this before, Pete! I don't understand it."

He took his arm away. "Well, you've never acted like this before. I mean, making a big deal over Mario. I've got to know which one of us you want. Him or me. You've got to choose. *Now.*"

Donna felt a lump in her throat, and the thudding in her temples seemed loud enough for him to hear. She wished she sounded more convincing as she lashed back.

"You're nuts, you know that? I'm too busy to think about you, or Mario, or anyone. If you don't understand, it's your problem."

Was she actually speaking these words? And were they the truth? Did Mario actually mean nothing to her? And what about her feeling for Pete? What had happened to that?

Suddenly it was all too much. A lump in her throat exploded into a sob. She dropped her head into her hands and the tears came, even as she hated herself for letting her self-control crack this way.

Pete grabbed her hand and held it while he spoke to her in a low voice. "Don't cry, Donna. I didn't mean to be hard on you. I should've realized you're under a terrific strain." He was still soothing Donna, his comforting arm around her shoulder, when Abbey returned.

"Well, well! If it isn't Romeo and Juliet time again. All you need is a balcony." She sat down. "All I need is my pizza." Then she saw Donna's face, with the trace of tears still rimming her eyes. "Donna! What is it? Pete! Did you do this to her?"

"No, no! He didn't," Donna said. "I'm sorry. I apologize to both of you. It wasn't Pete's fault, Abbey. It wasn't anyone's fault." She looked at them, puzzled. "I don't know what happened. I just started to cry." She punched her fist on the table. "If there's anything I hate, it's anyone bursting into tears to get out of something." She wiped her eyes with the back of her hand. "You deserve an answer, Pete. Just give me a few more days. Can you do that?"

"I guess I can," Pete said.

"Can we get this show on the road?" Abbey asked. "Here comes the pizza!"

The next half hour went like old times, the three of them eating, talking, joking — almost like old times. But then all the jokes stopped, they paid their bill, and when Abbey and Donna said good-bye to Pete and left Pagano's, Donna felt that Pete was still hurt and angry.

They walked back in the dusk to the parking lot and stopped, shocked, when they saw it.

The red Mustang was where they'd left it. But the tires were flat on the cement. Someone had viciously, deliberately slashed all four of them.

THIRTEEN

"Now you're beginning to worry me," Mario Garcia said. "Anyone angry enough to risk being seen in a public place, methodically damaging all the tires on a car — anyone who does that means business. I got your parents calmed down because . . ."

"Don't say any more, Mario. I know what you mean," Donna said. The three of them — she, Mario, and Abbey — were in her apartment. The young detective had come at once when Donna phoned him from Pagano's. He had arranged for the car to be picked up and the tires repaired, and then drove both girls to Donna's place.

"What I'm trying to say," Mario continued, "is that this case has taken a nasty twist."

"I agree," Donna said. "Someone's got it in for me. But I'm not about to quit, Mario."

"I was afraid you'd say that. Which brings us to the question of — who?"

"Mario, have the police got any idea at all of how those parallel bars happened to land on Rick Roberts?" Donna sat down beside him on the sofa.

"The way we figure it, the rope that held the bars must have been put on the wrong hook up above in the rafters, *or* it was on the right hook but slipped off somehow and came down right where Rick was standing. Accidentally or on purpose." He looked grimly at her. "It makes Howard Reilly our hottest suspect. If only we could talk to him. . . ."

"I don't see why you're so convinced it was Mr. Reilly," Donna said. "Maybe Rick Roberts was in the wrong place. Or maybe someone besides Howard Reilly arranged for the rope to slip or ravel or whatever. . . ."

"Maybe." Mario sounded dubious. "But Rick was in the right place. You know, they mark the spot where someone is supposed to stand by putting a cross made out of blue adhesive tape on the floor. Everyone claims Rick was standing on that tape." He shook his head. "I'm afraid it was Reilly's fault, one way or the other. He's either a murderer, or like Rick Roberts said, he was just too old for the job."

Just then the house phone rang. Abbey jumped up and answered it before Donna could stop her. "Hello? Hello?" she said. "Who? Oh, Pete!" She looked over at Donna.

As Donna began to shake her head *no* vigorously, Abbey said, "Sure, come on up! Always room for one more!" and hung up.

Donna said angrily, "I wish you hadn't done that, Abbey." Then, as both Mario and Abbey stared at her, she blushed. "I mean, I just wanted space to think." It sounded limp even to her.

Footsteps sounded outside and then a knock on the door, and all at once Donna knew why she was feeling so much pressure. It wasn't just that she was getting nowhere on the Rick Roberts case. She was used to that kind of pressure and usually enjoyed it. No, it was something else. *It's Pete. He's the one making me feel like this, forcing me to make a choice I'm not ready for.*

She was actually frightened at the thought of what Pete would think when he found Mario there. Then common sense returned. *I can't live in fear of Pete. It's childish and stupid and I won't do it.*

In the next minute, Abbey flung the door open and Pete stood there in the doorway. His eyes scanned the room and landed on Mario Garcia.

"I didn't know you had company," he said quietly.

Instantly Abbey said, "Come in, Pete. Don't stand there." She pulled him into the room. "Wait'll you hear what happened! Mario came to the rescue."

"Sit down, Pete." Mario Garcia gestured

toward a chair. "This case is getting warmer and warmer — in fact, it's practically hot."

"Want something to eat?" Abbey asked Pete. "And by the way, what are you doing here?"

"Don't be rude," Donna said. "Pete's always welcome." *I hope he'll buy that,* Donna thought. *I can't stand any hassle from him now. Not now.*

"Want to tell me how the investigation is going?" Pete asked Mario directly. "Or is it top secret?"

"Not in your case," Mario said. "We think Howard Reilly may be our man, but we can't do anything about it, not until he comes out of his unconscious state."

Mario looked at his watch. "I don't believe it! I've got a couple of suspects in an arson case waiting at headquarters. Captain Gavin will have my head." He opened a notebook, took out a sheet of paper, and thrust it at Donna. "Here! I ran off these notes for you, kid. Maybe they'll come in handy." He hurried to the door, where he turned, said goodbye to Pete and Abbey, and blew a kiss at Donna. He was gone in a flash.

Donna picked up the sheet of paper that Mario had left. "This is a complete rundown of where the police stand. Nothing new as far as I can see. But it's got the names and addresses of Abe Hazelkorn, Rex Vicente, David Gould . . . everyone. That was really sweet of Mario."

Donna glanced at Pete and saw him looking at her appraisingly. Again he seemed like a stranger. "I'm sorry, Pete." She ran a hand through her hair. "I'm so tied up in this case, it's all I can think about. I wonder why?"

"Yeah. I wonder why, too." As he saw Abbey disappear into the hallway he said, "Thanks, Donna."

Surprised, she asked, "Thanks for what, Pete?"

He took two steps toward the door, then turned back, his face an accustomed, inexpressive mask. "Thanks for calling Mario Garcia instead of me when you were in trouble. It lets me know how I rate with you."

Donna's hazel eyes flashed angrily. "You don't know what you're saying, Pete. And I don't have the time or patience to argue with you."

"I phoned because I thought we could talk things over. But it's too late." He waved his hand. "Well, see you around — but I doubt it. Good-bye!"

He walked out and slammed the door behind him. Abbey, coming over with their pajamas, saw a very upset sister standing there.

"What was that all about?" she demanded. "I couldn't hear what the two of you were saying."

"Not now." Donna reached for her pajamas, still too hurt and bewildered by Pete's rough treatment to talk about it. She got into bed. But when she put out the light, she saw

Pete's angry face once more. She couldn't believe it — why, they'd known each other for almost four years. *How could he do this to me?* she thought. *I can't stand it.*

The next day, Sunday, Donna called Abe Hazelkorn and asked if she could come to see him. He graciously invited Donna and Abbey for brunch. At noon, Donna and Abbey walked into the elegant lobby of Abe Hazelkorn's apartment house. A gloriously outfitted doorman announced them and minutes later they were at apartment 14-B and Abe Hazelkorn was smiling warmly.

"Good afternoon, Mr. Hazelkorn. It was so nice of you to invite us to brunch," Donna said.

"My pleasure. Come in, both of you," he said, beaming at Abbey.

They followed him into a large living room with a wall of wide windows overlooking the park.

"I hope I can help," he said. "Please have a seat or look at the view, and I'll get the food on. I hope you're hungry."

He left, and the two girls took a look around the beautifully furnished room. A blue velvet sofa was flanked by two walnut tables facing a huge brick fireplace. In one corner there was a baby grand piano with a stack of music books on the side.

"Abbey," Donna whispered, "go over and look at the piano. I'll take the bookcases. If he catches you, you can say . . ."

"Don't tell me what to say," Abbey whispered back. "I can handle it."

Abbey hurried across to the piano while Donna began to search the wall of books above the fireplace to see if there was anything of interest there. Abe Hazelkorn was obviously deeply immersed in show business. There were pictures against the wall between the shelves — pictures of celebrities from the theater world, from films and, of course, from TV. But by and large, most of the pictures were of movie stars. Donna was surprised to see that a picture was missing from the wall. There was a solitary nail and beneath it the clear rectangular space, slightly lighter than the wall surrounding it, from which a picture had obviously been removed.

Donna crossed over to the piano and Abbey stepped aside to make room for her. At that moment, Abe Hazelkorn was coming down a hallway outside the room — they could hear his footsteps on the polished wood floor. Abbey, in her haste, knocked over the pile of music books.

"Oh, murder! What did I do?" she muttered as Donna bent down and started to scoop up the books. From between the books, a glass-framed photo slipped out, and Donna saw a portrait of Lana Lawrence. She just had time to read the inscription at the bottom: TO ABE, WITH LOVE, LANA.

"Hurry, he's coming!" Abbey whispered. Donna barely had time to thrust the picture back and restore the music pile to the top of the piano, before the producer entered the room pushing a serving cart laden with food.

"Can we help?" Donna asked.

"Just serve yourselves." He indicated the lavish spread, the center of which was a silver platter with a whole sizzling fish.

"Do you mind if I skip the fish?" Abbey said. "You've got such goodies here, I adore them. And I — I'm not too fond of most fish."

"Try just a little," Mr. Hazelkorn said. "I think you may like it. It's only this time of year that you can get it. It's flown in to me from near the Canadian border. Here, let me give you some."

Donna cast a warning look at Abbey, who reluctantly lifted her fork and daintily pierced a small piece of the sizzling hot fish.

"Careful," the producer said. "Give it a second to cool. Try it, Abbey. Don't be afraid."

Abbey waved the fork gently above her plate, then could delay no longer. As she tasted, her eyes popped wide open. She turned to their host, who was watching her with genuine pleasure."

"Oh, it's superb!" she said. "Donna, taste it, taste it! Food for the gods!"

"I'm glad you like it," the producer said. "It's a very difficult fish to catch. It's brown spotted trout, for which you need a special lure, and it's mostly found in certain northern lakes where they have to cut a hole in the ice to get to the fish." He stopped. "What's the matter, Donna?" he asked.

Donna, who had been staring at him with

a faraway look, shook her head. "I'm sorry. I was just thinking of something."

Abbey quickly said, "This food is delicious. You're a gourmet cook, Mr. Hazelkorn."

He flushed with pleasure. "Thank you, Abbey. But I'm sure your sister would like to get down to business."

"Oh, not now," Donna said. "Let's enjoy this marvelous meal first, Mr. Hazelkorn. It's sensational."

The producer was pleased, and the three spent the next hour talking, laughing, and enjoying the delicious food. But at last the meal ended, and Abe Hazelkorn turned to Donna.

"Start talking," he said. "I'm ready to tell you anything I can."

"All right." Donna pushed her plate away and leaned toward him. "Three questions, Mr. Hazelkorn. One, do you think what happened to Rick was an accident?"

The producer was instantly serious. "Nothing like that has ever happened in my experience. Not in TV. We handle too much heavy equipment to risk anything like that." He shook his head. "Howard Reilly was about the best there is in the business. I can't see Howard overlooking the least precaution in setting up a stunt like the one Rick was supposed to do that day. The man's too experienced."

"But he got very sick right afterward," Donna said. "Maybe he wasn't feeling well while he was setting the equipment up."

"If he didn't feel well, Howard Reilly would be the first one to say so and ask for someone else to handle the job." Hazelkorn's lips tightened. "It couldn't have been an accident with Howard."

"Could he have done it — on purpose?" Donna asked.

"Anything is possible." The producer shrugged. "What's the next question?"

"What did David Gould hand you at the cemetery, Mr. Hazelkorn?" The question came out with the force of a bullet at Mr. Hazelkorn.

He flushed darkly and said, "Why don't you ask David Gould? It's not for me to say."

"Can't you tell me anything about it?" Donna said. "It looked like the small black plastic box they put a cassette in." She waited. He was considering the matter.

"You're right, Donna. But that's all I'm going to tell you. Gould can fill you in on the rest if he wants to." He stood up. "You said there was a third question?"

Donna hesitated. "Lana Lawrence . . ." she said slowly. As Hazelkorn's face went a deep red, she said, "Was Lana Lawrence angry enough at Rick to have done something about it?"

"Lana was treated very badly by Rick. He was the star of my show. But I tell you, he was capable of great cruelty." He looked squarely at Donna. "Sure, I guess Lana had plenty of reason to hate him. But so did a lot of other people. I don't want to say any more.

I'm sorry Rick died — and I hope that the police will find out why." He looked at his watch.

"Thank you for everything," Donna said.

"One more thing." Abe Hazelkorn was speaking directly to Donna now. "I am extremely anxious to get this case solved. It's interfering with production at the studio, and we owe it to Rick to clear this matter up." He cleared his throat. "I have a great deal of respect for you, Donna. And — how shall I say it? — I realize that as a student, you don't have a great source of funds at your disposal. If you should need any money in your investigation, please call on me."

"That's very kind of you," Donna said, wondering, *Is this a cover-up, Mr. Hazelkorn? Are you trying to buy me off?*

"Don't thank me. Television has been very good to me. It doesn't hurt for me to give some back." The producer held out his hand.

"We'll be going now," Donna said, shaking his hand.

"I'll never forget your sensational meal," Abbey said, blinking her long black lashes. "Especially the trout. It's made a fish eater out of me."

The moment they got outside, Abbey said, "Okay, tell me. Tell me right away!"

"Tell you what?" Donna asked as they walked to the car.

"You know darn well," Abbey said. "Something happened up there at Hazelkorn's apartment that got to you. Either that or you had one of your blinding flashes. I want to know, Donna."

"All right, I'll tell you, Abbey. I *think* I have an idea of where Johnny Argyle is." Donna opened the door of the car and the two girls got in.

"Where?" Abbey demanded. "I can't stand the suspense."

"You're going to have to stand it." Donna revved up the motor. "I won't really know anything until I make a few phone calls."

"It isn't fair." Abbey sulked as the car wended its way through the Sunday traffic. "You never tell me everything. You always hold something back."

Donna looked briefly at her sister. "You know why, Abbey. I always want your instinctive, unprejudiced reaction. The more you know, the less instinctive it is."

"All right," Abbey grumbled, secretly pleased by her sister's opinion. "I suppose there's no use asking you where we're going next?"

"Don't be silly. Our first stop is Twenty-eight Oak Leaf Road. Rex Vicente's house."

"And the next place?"

Donna swung the car out of the slow traffic lane. "You'll see. Not now, not in this traffic."

"You see? I knew it! You're doing it again!" Abbey stared grumpily out the window all the way to Oak Leaf Road.

When they came up the snow-shoveled walk to the lovely white house with green shutters, they heard the strains of "Amaryllis," the charming eighteenth-century French minuet, coming from inside.

"That's 'Amaryllis,'" Abbey said. "And a real weird orchestra playing. Not a very professional one."

Donna rang the doorbell and the music inside stopped. The front door opened and the maestro of "The Teenage Talent Show" blinked behind horn-rimmed glasses. He was carrying a baton in one hand and was dressed casually in an open-necked, soft beige shirt with a flowing brown ascot tie. He looked at them indecisively for a moment, then smiled.

"Miss Rockford! What a pleasant surprise! Come in!" He stepped aside to allow the two girls to enter. Before them was a spacious room, which at the moment was fully occupied by an assortment of musicians, ranging from five years of age to an elderly man in his seventies. All looked expectantly at the newcomers.

"This is the Oak Leaf Road Sunday Symphony Orchestra," he said. "The cellist" — he indicated the old man — "is my father, Richard Vicente. The beautiful woman at the piano is my wife, Dolores. The violinists and flutist and oboist are my children and their friends. We do this every week and the neighbors are very understanding. They haven't thrown any tomatoes yet or called the police."

At the mention of the last word, his face

grew serious. "Would you like to speak to me, Miss Rockford?"

"It won't take long," Donna said.

"Try that last allegro part again," he called into the living room. "And you two young ladies come with me. I hope you don't mind the kitchen."

For the next ten minutes, Rex Vicente told them all he knew about Rick Roberts and the show. "I'd be less than honest if I didn't tell you that I resented the way Rick treated me," he said. "That nickname — 'The Wreck' — is an example." He shook his head somberly, remembering.

"Do you know anyone who might have wanted to kill Rick?" Donna asked. "Do you think his death was accidental?"

"Plenty of people had reason to hate him, Miss Rockford. And I don't know how it could have been an accident."

"Daddy, Sharon says you hold the E-flat in the third bar. That isn't right, is it?" A tousle-haired boy of about eight, looking like a Xerox copy of his father and carrying an undersized violin, waited for a reply.

"We won't keep you any longer," Donna said. "You've been very kind."

Abbey said to the small boy, "You don't hold the first E-flat. It's the second one that gets the *sustenuto*."

"Well, so you're a musician! How bright of you!" Mr. Vicente said. "What instrument do you play?"

"Mostly the guitar," Abbey said, flushed with joy at the compliment.

Outside, in the car, Donna turned to Abbey. "How in the world did you know that — about the music, I mean?"

"One shot in a million," Abbey said. "Some kid in my class at Juilliet last year made the same mistake. That's the one and only bit of expertise I picked up." She shifted in her seat as the car headed toward the heart of town. "What's the next stop?"

"David Gould's house." Donna turned on the heater. "*Brrr*. I'm cold," she said.

Abbey took off her red wool scarf and draped it over her sister's shoulders. "It's old age. It's coming on you all at once." Then she took a closer look at her sister. "Uh-oh. You're excited. The trail's getting hot, right?"

"Hotter than I expected, Abbey." She braked the car before a low, fairly rickety brownstone house. "This is it. Let's have a word with Mr. Gould."

David Gould's home looked like the laboratory of a mad inventor. Tables, shelves, even the floor of one room, were cluttered with every conceivable kind of audio equipment imaginable. There were stereos, the latest in hi-fi equipment, and then a range of disks, tapes, microphones, bullhorns — any and everything that made any sort of sound, including a wonderful old early phonograph of which the plump audio man was inordinately proud.

"They made that machine in eighteen

ninety-two," he said. "Look at this record. It's all metal — a museum piece. Want to hear it play?"

Donna thanked him. "There isn't time. I have just a few questions I'd like to ask you, Mr. Gould."

"Go right ahead," he said cautiously.

First she asked the usual questions and got the same responses. Rick Roberts had enemies, an accident seemed unlikely, and last, he had no idea who could have killed Rick.

"Mr. Gould, you handed something to Mr. Hazelkorn at the funeral services," Donna said, plunging right in. "Want to tell me what it was?"

"I can't tell you that." The man's jolly, round face lost its warmth and he was unfriendly and impatient. "Will that be all?"

Two minutes later they were back in the car.

"Let's head for home," Donna said. "If you want any food or anything, let's stop and get it now."

"Stop at the Rialto Delicatessen," Abbey said. "Just leave it all to me."

Ten minutes later a triumphant Abbey emerged from the store with a huge brown bag that filled the car with tantalizing aromas.

"Pastrami, corned beef, pickles, cole slaw, big, fat special frankfurters. Oh, hurry, before I pass out," she said.

"Hold up a moment." Donna suddenly swung the car down a familiar street.

"Don't tell me." Abbey groaned. "We're stopping at police headquarters."

"I've got to talk to Dr. Rosen," Donna said. "He may already have that report on Lana's perfume, if we're lucky."

They were lucky.

"It just came in," the police physician said, handing a handwritten report to Donna. "I haven't even had a chance to type it up yet. It's all yours, Donna."

"Thank you, Dr. Rosen. This is terrific." Donna seized the paper eagerly. At the top, it read: "Higrade Chemists. Product: Perfume. Type: 'Seduction.' Customer: Lana Lawrence, Actress, Hollywood."

No surprises there. And then the last line that blazed across the page like a flash of lightning: *"December tenth, ten-ounce bottle sent to Miss Lawrence, billed to Mr. Abe Hazelkorn. $6,000.00."*

FOURTEEN

"Where are you going?" Abbey demanded, as her sister made for the exit stairway.

"I want to try to catch Mario, if he's still here." Donna took the stairs two at a time going down, then hurried to the homicide division and pushed the door open.

Mario Garcia was just taking his hat off a coatrack as they came in.

"Donna! Abbey! What a surprise!" Mario said. "But I can't spend any time with you."

"What's the big rush?" Donna asked.

He hesitated, then said, "I can't keep any information from you, not after all the legwork you've done." Mario buckled his trenchcoat and took her arm and Abbey's as he headed out of the office. "There's been a break in the case. I just got word from the hospital. Howard Reilly has regained consciousness and there's a good chance that I can talk to him."

"That's wonderful!" Donna said. "You're going to let me go with you, aren't you?"

"It won't be a picnic," Mario said. "He's still not out of the woods."

"How about me?" Abbey said. "Can't I go, too?"

"On one condition," Mario said. "You stay downstairs in the reception room. Got that?"

"And you wait right there for us," Donna said. "You don't stir one inch away, understand?"

"Stop nagging, both of you," Abbey implored. "You'll drive me straight to the psychiatric division."

"Or vice versa," Donna said. They spent the rest of the trip to the hospital in silence.

Once in the lighted lobby of the hospital, Donna said, "This case is racing to a conclusion and we can't slow the pace."

"It is?" Mario looked at her curiously. "What have you got, Donna?"

"It can wait," Donna said, as they left Abbey behind in the reception area. She hurriedly followed Mario into an elevator marked FOR STAFF ONLY.

"The patient in six-oh-nine cannot be disturbed," the nurse said.

"I'm the police," Detective Garcia said, showing his badge under his lapel. "We've heard that Mr. Reilly regained consciousness. All we want is a word with him."

The nurse stood tall and straight and unyielding as a stone wall. "You'll have to speak to his physician, then. I can't possibly violate the rules."

Minutes later, a dark-skinned man in his thirties approached quickly down the corridor. A tag on his jacket said JOHN BARONE, M.D.

"Can I help you? I understand you would like to visit Mr. Reilly, but I'm afraid that's not possible. He has some mobility, but he can't speak. He's in a very precarious state still."

"He wouldn't have to speak," Mario said. "I wouldn't ask this, doctor, but it's a question of a murder investigation. If I could just have a minute or two with him."

The doctor looked at him dubiously. "It's not the sort of request I'd ever agree to, Detective Garcia. But yours is a special case, I suppose." He looked at his watch. "Just a few minutes, you said? Follow me."

Donna and Mario followed the doctor as he gently opened the door of Room 609. It was a small room with a single bed, a washstand, a chest of drawers.

Howard Reilly lay in the bed with his eyes closed. If he heard them enter the room, he gave no sign of it. The doctor motioned Mario Garcia and Donna to come close. That was when they saw, for the first time, that Bonnie Reilly was in the room. She was sitting in a chair in a niche beside a wardrobe closet and had not seen them till just this moment. She jumped up quickly and motioned them away.

"No, no!" she said in a low voice, angrily. "You can't come in. Get out!"

"This man is from the police, Miss Reilly," the doctor said. "I've given permission for him to ask your father a few questions."

Bonnie crossed to the bed and stood in front of where her father lay. Her eyes glittered threateningly, as she sought to keep them from coming nearer.

"I won't let you," she said. "He's my father! That gives me the right to keep anyone away, even the police."

"I'm sorry to say that isn't true," the doctor said. "If anyone has my permission — and Detective Garcia does — you can't stop him."

"I'm sure you don't want to hinder any investigation into Rick Roberts' death," Mario said. "Just a few words with your father, and we won't have to bother either of you again."

Bonnie surveyed Mario intently. "Is that a promise?" she said.

"It certainly is," Mario said carefully. "And I don't break promises."

The young girl took a deep breath, then said, "I'll hold you to that, Detective Garcia." She stepped aside to let him come near. Then she bent down to her father and said softly, "Daddy. It's Bonnie."

The man in the bed slowly opened his

eyes. He looked at first as if he were half asleep, but then he focused on his daughter's face.

She squeezed his hand lovingly and said, "This man is a detective. He wants to ask you a few questions. Do you feel strong enough to answer? Just tap my hand for yes."

At the word "detective," Mr. Reilly's eyes shifted to Mario, then to Donna. Again he seemed to be half dreaming. Then he slowly raised his forefinger and tapped his daughter's hand.

Mario came near and said, "Thank you, Mr. Reilly. This will just take a minute. I only want to ask you about what happened last Wednesday on the show. . . ."

The man's eyes showed his alarm. He looked at his daughter, as if for consent. When she nodded, he turned back to Mario.

"I'll just ask you one question." Mario came closer to Howard Reilly and knelt beside him. "I'll call off the names of people. When I come to the person you believe was responsible for the accident, just tap your daughter's hand. Can you do that?"

Again Mr. Reilly's eyes sought his daughter. Again she nodded her consent — much more reluctantly this time, Donna thought. Howard Reilly lifted his forefinger and tapped his daughter's hand.

The doctor, who had been watching carefully, said quickly, "I don't think he's up to this. . . ."

In exactly that instant, the sick man said,

in a voice like a frog's croak, barely intelligible, "John-ny . . . Ar. . . ." Overcome by the effort, Howard Reilly suddenly closed his eyes.

"He can speak!" the doctor said. He immediately hurried over, lifted the man's wrist, and felt his pulse. Then he looked at the others. "He's all right. Your question, Detective Garcia, probably sparked his voice processes. But he's very weak — I cannot allow any more questions. Sorry."

Bonnie said indignantly, "My father is confused! He didn't know what he was saying!"

Detective Garcia said, "I'm very sorry that we had to disturb him, Miss Reilly. We're leaving now."

In the corridor, Donna said, "I'm glad he's going to recover. He seems to be such a nice person." As they went through the revolving doors downstairs, Donna asked Mario, "What do you think, Mario? Do you believe what Howard Reilly said? That Johnny Argyle was responsible for what happened to Rick?"

"Could be," Mario said grimly. "This case might be sewed up in ten seconds flat — if I could only locate Johnny Argyle."

They were now in the detective's unmarked police car, with Abbey, heading for Donna's apartment. Mario drove carefully, intent on the road, which was coated with a film of ice.

"If I could just lay my hands on that Argyle kid. No one has any idea where he went. Isn't that incredible?"

"Would you like to know where he might be?" Donna asked.

Mario almost let go of the steering wheel as he spun his head in Donna's direction. "Are you serious?"

"Mario! Keep your eyes on the road, for heaven's sake." Donna grabbed the wheel to steady it. "I'm not positive, but I think I know where Johnny Argyle may be holing up."

Again Mario reacted by looking off the icy road, but corrected himself in time. Staring straight through the windshield at the heavy traffic ahead, he said, between clenched teeth, "Tell me, Donna. Don't play games."

"Abbey and I had brunch at Abe Hazelkorn's house today. He served us a fish that he says comes from near the Canadian border. Well, Minnesota is near the Canadian border. . . . Mario, don't ask questions. Just let me make a few phone calls, and I think there's a good possibility you can get hold of Johnny Argyle in the next twenty-four hours."

"I can't believe this," Mario said. "How can you be so sure? Have you got the inside track on something? And where did you get it?" He straightened behind the wheel of the car. "You know, I'm the police."

"Don't be dense, Mario," Abbey said from the backseat of the car. "You know, she gets these fits, and then when she comes out of it, she's had a revelation."

"Congratulations, Abbey. You've managed to insult both of us at the same time," Donna said. "I don't mind — but Mario is *not* your buddy, Abbey."

"I'm sorry, Mario. I won't do it again — I hope," Abbey said.

"Hello, Mr. Hazelkorn? This is Donna Rockford. . . ." As Donna saw Abbey approach the phone booth on the corner outside her dorm building, she pulled the door shut and spoke in a voice too low for Abbey to overhear what was being said.

Abbey stood impatiently tapping her foot as she waited for the frustrating conversation to end. At last, Donna emerged from the booth, with a wicked gleam in her eye.

"Why couldn't I listen?" Abbey said. "What am I all of a sudden, poison or something?"

"Not to Mr. Hazelkorn, you aren't," Donna said. "He's so fond of you, Abbey, that when I asked him if he meant what he said about paying any expenses on this case, he said, 'Anything for Abbey's sister,' and then agreed to pay my expenses for a trip to Minnesota with Mario."

"Honestly? He said that?" Abbey was elated. "What a nice man! If only he were thirty years younger. . . ."

"That wasn't all he said." Donna looked knowingly at Abbey. "He also mentioned that if I needed you to help me solve this case, and if you had the slightest desire to take a little trip. . . ."

Abbey grabbed her sister. "I don't believe it! You mean he said — he said —" Her breath choked in her throat and she couldn't go on.

"He's going to pay my fare and yours to Minnesota!"

"*Yippee!*" Abbey began to swing her sister in a mad whirl that resembled a polka, while several passersby stopped to enjoy the sight of two great-looking teenagers cavorting amid the falling snow.

Donna pulled Abbey to a halt and said, "I've got one more phone call to make, and you can listen to this one."

She went back into the booth and dialed the police precinct. With Abbey leaning close to her sister's cheek to hear both sides of the conversation, Donna said, "Hello, Mario? Donna. I phoned a friend and everything's all arranged. What's that? Yes, it was Abe Hazelkorn . . . and make that three tickets. . . . Yes, Mario" — she winked at her sister — "he's treating Abbey, too. Some kid, huh? And Mario, one more bulletin — Mr. Hazelkorn told me that Lana Lawrence just came back to town. . . . Yes, the Stanton Savoy. . . . I thought you'd be interested. . . . Well, see you in the airport at seven o'clock."

"So it's Johnny Argyle, after all?" Abbey said, as they headed down the street.

"Not now," Donna said, an unhappy look settling on her face. "We've got less than an hour to pack for Minnesota."

The airport was bustling at seven o'clock. Passengers crowded the terminal. Detective

Garcia greeted the two girls as they came through the electrically powered doors and took their overnight bags.

"Let's not waste any time," he said. He turned to Donna. "I'm not sure it's such a bright idea taking the kid along." Abbey snorted, but said nothing.

"We didn't have much choice," Donna said. "With my parents off in Georgia, I wouldn't be happy being fifteen or eighteen hundred miles away from Abbey myself."

"And of course you have to come along, Donna," Mario said.

"Of course." Donna smiled jauntily at him.

Mario had tried to sound stern, but he melted and looked admiringly at Donna as the three of them stood in line before the desk where an attendant was assigning seat locations for the flight.

"Can I get some chocolate?" Abbey asked. "It'll just take a minute, and you two can keep my place in line. I'm a white-knuckle flier — it'll quiet my nerves."

Without waiting for an answer, she turned and sped to the nearest candy-and-magazine shop, where she grabbed a king-size chocolate bar. She was paying for it when she saw a familiar figure passing by.

It was Pete O'Brien, with an older man. He walked toward Abbey. "My grandfather," he said. "What are you doing here?"

Unconsciously, Abbey shifted her eyes to where, halfway across the tremendous ticket-ing area, Donna was talking animatedly with Mario Garcia, who chose that moment to laugh and pat Donna's cheek.

"Is that who I think it is?" Pete nodded toward Donna and Mario.

"Yes, Pete. But it's not what you think," Abbey said as Pete started to leave.

"Nice try, Abbey," he called back.

Abbey yelled, "Pete! You're making a mistake!" But he was gone.

When Abbey returned to the waiting line, she whispered to Donna, "You'll never believe who I just saw."

"Oh, yes, I will," Donna said unhappily, also whispering. "My ex-boyfriend. Who was that with him?"

Abbey told her and before they could say anymore, it was time to board the plane.

They jetted off into the dark night sky a half hour later. Normally, Abbey would have been excited, even ecstatic, by the flight westward. But Donna, sitting beside her and looking out the window with brooding eyes, was so obviously engrossed in her thoughts that Abbey left her alone, and contented herself with reading the gossip magazines the steward brought her.

Once Abbey looked up and saw her sister furtively wipe a tear from the corner of her eye. Abbey wondered, *What's she upset about? Is it only Pete? Or is she feeling guilty about leading Detective Mario Garcia to Johnny Argyle?*

When they got off the plane in Minnesota, there was a waiting jeep, lettered on the side RYAN'S FISHING CAMP, VOYAGEUR STATE PARK.

The driver, a grizzled but hearty-looking man in a rough lumber jacket and heavy rubber boots, looked at them curiously as the other passengers streamed away in different directions. Finally he came over to them.

"You the people who called from Philadelphia? Detective Mario Garcia?" He examined Mario's police ID and nodded. "Follow me."

The jeep sped them along the narrow road that led off the broad express highway, and soon they were traveling through a forest, with trees so tall and densely rooted that the snow weighting their branches barely sifted down to the ground below.

"*Brrr.*" Abbey shivered, pulled her down jacket close about her, and wrapped her wool muffler around her neck and ears. "It's *cold* up here."

The driver smiled briefly at her. "Yup. Twenty below this very minute — with a windchill factor of fifty below."

Detective Garcia said, "Have you been able to locate the Argyle boy? Or wouldn't you be the one to know about it?"

"I'm the one all right. I'm Jim Ryan. But like I told you, folks rent boats from me and take 'em out wherever they want. Some head upstream two or three days away from my place."

"How do they manage? It must be real wilderness," Donna said.

Mr. Ryan looked at her appreciatively in the mirror over the windshield. "You can say that again, young lady. They go to one of the cabins up there, and they've got no running water, no electricity, nothing but fishing." He cleared his throat. "And that's why they come here. They want to get away from the telephone, the radio, the TV, all that unnatural stuff that city people have gotten themselves used to, things folks were never meant to have."

"I understand why you couldn't take time out to look for him," Mario said, "but the rangers could use a helicopter, isn't that right?"

"This time of year, we don't call them out unless it's an emergency," Mr. Ryan said. "I thought you told me not to bother. Didn't you say you were coming out yourself?"

"How early in the morning will we be able to start looking for Johnny Argyle?" Mario Garcia said.

"Not much before sunup," Jim Ryan said. "It's too dark, too cold. Whatever sunshine hits the river, it helps warm things up."

Ryan's camp consisted of a main building and six small wooden shacks, with a small building in the fear for washing and bathroom facilities.

"This is dismal," Abbey whispered as Mr. Ryan flung open the door of one of the shacks.

"You girls can bunk here tonight," he said, indicating two army cots side by side in a space barely big enough for them. There were two sleeping bags on one of the cots as well as a pile of old woolen blankets.

"You come with me, Detective Garcia," he said, and in a minute the two girls were left alone in the freezing little cabin.

"We won't live through the night," Abbey prophesied. "We'll be two blocks of ice by morning."

"Sleep with your clothes on," Donna said. "Just take your boots off."

Mollified, Abbey soon got into her sleeping bag. "How in the world did you figure out that Johnny Argyle was in this crazy place?" Abbey asked, her teeth chattering.

"When we visited his mother," Donna said, "there was a note on his bulletin board that said the date of his vacation and the word 'Voyage!' and that didn't make sense."

"So why didn't you quit while you were ahead?" Abbey grumbled.

"But when I realized I had seen a pink plastic fish lure on his father's picture, and Johnny came from Minnesota, and so does brown-spotted trout, especially near a state park named Voyageur. . . ."

"I get it. If only you weren't such a genius, we'd both live to a ripe old age, instead of freezing to death in the wilderness." She groaned. "It was great knowing you, Donna." She pulled half a dozen blankets over her, made a tent of one quilt over her head, and fell fast asleep.

Donna lay in the dark, suffering. If things had been hopeless with Pete before, there was surely no saving their relationship now. Too much had happened. It made a cold lump of sorrow inside her.

And that wasn't all. She wondered how poor Mr. Reilly was doing back home in Philadelphia.

Her last thoughts were of what tomorrow would bring. They would search for Johnny Argyle, and if they found him, what would happen then?

As if in answer to her question, from far off in the distance there came the high, keening wail of a lonely coyote.

"Get up! Time to rise and shine!"

Mario was pounding on the door as he called to them.

From under her mountain of covers, Abbey let out a groan. A moment later she peered out. "It can't be time to get up already," she said.

"But it is. As a matter of fact" — Donna looked at her wristwatch — "it's five o'clock." A wicked impulse made her reach over and pull the blankets off her sister. "Come on, Abbey. We've got to go out to that washroom and at least brush our teeth."

"What with? Ice cubes?" Abbey swung her feet out of the sleeping bag and got up. "I would like to say that this was the worst night I've ever spent, but" — she broke into a foolish smile — "I had the most sensational sleep of all time."

The air was bracing as they went to Mr. Ryan's main office and smelled bacon and eggs and pancakes and coffee inside. A crude, long wooden table was already set, and Jim Ryan was taking their plates from atop a wood stove that looked very old and burned very hot.

"One of the men came back from upriver last night. I asked him if he'd seen Johnny Argyle, but he claims there wasn't a living soul about."

"The Mohunk River is famous for its brown-spotted trout, isn't it?" Donna asked.

"It is that," Mr. Ryan agreed, "but there's not too many of them around, this time of year. Still, you never can tell." He scratched his scraggly beard. "A body's got to be a little teched to come looking for brown trout in the dead of winter."

"Either that, or it's a great excuse to get away from trouble someplace else," Mario offered gratuitously.

As Mr. Ryan flashed a curious look at Mario, Donna quickly said, "Don't pay any attention, Mr. Ryan. As far as we know, Johnny Argyle hasn't done anything wrong."

Mario said, "As far as we know." He got up and started for the door. "I'll load the boat and then you two had better be ready to leave."

"We'll give you a hand," Donna said, following him out.

"Too bad I can't go with you," Mr. Ryan said. "I'm expecting my supplies for the next two months, and I'd better be here to get them."

A half hour later, Mario, Donna, and Abbey started upstream on the Mohunk in a tidy little craft with a powerful motor.

"There's plenty to keep you warm and plenty to keep you fed for a whole week," Mr. Ryan reminded them. "If anything goes wrong, send up some flares and the forest rangers will find you. Just don't wait too long to ask for help."

The sun was just showing its tip as they putt-putted up the rapidly flowing river. The golden gleam on the waters was a sight so beautiful, all three sailed silently along, absorbing the magic splendor. But while Abbey *ooh*'d and *aah*'d in wonderment, both Donna and Mario began to search the shoreline for signs of life.

Hours later, snow began to fall heavily and Mario headed for shore.

"This is a risky business, and I'm not going to endanger either you or Abbey," Mario told Donna.

She made no protest. Half of her was hoping they would not find Johnny Argyle. Donna hated to think of what would happen then — but there was nothing she could do to stop it.

They took shelter in the small clearing.

They quickly put up a tent, lined the ground inside with a plastic cover, and prepared to wait until the snowfall ended. While Donna and Mario set up a game of chess on a miniature board, Abbey grew restless.

"I'm getting claustrophobia in here," she said. "Mind if I take a breather outside?"

"Fine, but don't go more than ten feet away from this tent," Mario warned.

Donna and Mario continued their game, deeply concentrating, when suddenly they heard a wild yell from outside.

"That's Abbey!" Donna said, as she raced outside. An instant later, she grabbed Mario's arm as he came beside her.

"Look!" she said in a low voice. Mario looked to where she pointed and saw a bear on hind legs leaning against a tree and looking upward at someone.

It was Abbey.

FIFTEEN

High on a branch, Abbey was perched with legs dangling, her face white as the thin stream of snow that found its way through the trees.

Suddenly Mario burst out laughing. Donna stared at him. "Mario! My sister's life is in danger, and you laugh?"

"Cool it," Mario said. "Look at the collar on that bear. See the tag hanging from it? That means he's one of the park's tame bears." He stopped and called out, "Don't be afraid, Abbey! He won't hurt you. Just stay there!"

"D-d-don't worry," came Abbey's answer. "I'm f-frozen on this b-branch!"

"Go to the tent, Donna, and get the jar of

honey in the food bag. No sweat. This boy is just trying to be friendly."

In a minute Donna was back. Mario took the jar of honey and, holding it in front of him, began to make a little clucking noise.

"Here, boy. Here, boy," he called as if the big brown bear were a dog.

The bear looked around and saw him, saw what he was holding, and lowered his forelegs from the tree. Then, like a clumsy puppy, he waddled over. He looked at Donna and Mario quizzically; satisfied, he began to lick the honey Mario was holding. As he did, Mario led him toward a path in the woods from which he had probably come.

Donna ran to the base of the tree and called up to Abbey, "You can come down now. He's gone!"

There was no answer.

Donna looked up through the branches. Abbey was shielding her eyes from the snow's glare and squinting off in the distance.

"Abbey!" Donna yelled again. "You can come down now! What are you doing?"

Abbey grinned down at her sister through the tree's branches. "I climbed up here to get away from the bear. Now he's gone someplace else, so I've had a change in plans."

"What did you say?" Donna asked quietly.

"I said, the bear moved away, so I changed my plans. I want to stay here and enjoy the view a few minutes. Do you mind?"

"I don't mind, Abbey," Donna said. "Take a good look. Just don't slip and fall."

In that instant, Abbey yelled, "Donna! I think I see something — I do!" She started to bounce on the limb she was standing on. "Get me my opera glasses — they're in my bag!" She was jiggling up and down now.

"Stop that, Abbey, or you'll fall down," Donna warned.

Mario came running up. "What's going on?" he said.

From above, Abbey yelled, "Get my spy glasses — quick!"

Mario reached for the field glasses hanging about his neck on a leather strap, together with a miniature camera. "She can use these," Mario said, as Donna bent down and got a piece of dead branch about ten feet long.

"Here, take this," she said. "You can tie the glasses on it and pass them up to her."

Mario poked the long branch with the glasses tied to it up through the branches, and Abbey took them eagerly.

She took one long, piercing look through them. "It's a man in a red fishing jacket. I'll bet it's Johnny Argyle!" She said, "Here, catch!" and dropped the glasses down to Donna. Then she yelled, "Get ready, Mario — I'm coming down!"

She made her way down a few feet, stepping from branch to branch, then leaped into Mario's waiting arms.

"How did you ever make that first big jump into the tree?" Mario asked.

"You wouldn't ask that if you were the one

a bear was chasing," Abbey said. "It was sheer fright."

"How far off is the man you saw?" Mario asked.

"About a half mile away — in a straight line from here," Abbey said. "Maybe thirty yards in from the riverbank. There's a whole row of shorter trees, like the one I was on, and I could see past them. He's in a clearing. Come on, I'll take you there!"

"How about the boat?" Mario said.

"We don't need it. Let's go," Abbey insisted.

They made their way along the slippery, snow-covered riverbank, with Abbey leading them, using a branch as a walking stick. They walked silently; it took them twice as long to cover the distance because of the snow and ice underfoot. But at last they came to a clearing in the woods, and there they saw footsteps in the snow leading to a small inlet covered with ice.

Someone was fishing with a line dropped into a hole in the ice. He wore a red jacket and was concentrating deeply on the fishing line as it began to bob unevenly.

"Johnny Argyle?" Mario said.

The fisherman, still intent on the line, waved his hand to silence them. "Ssh! I've got a bite!" Suddenly he gave a yank at the line and began reeling it in quickly but carefully. A minute later, a brown-spotted fish about a foot and a half long appeared at the end of the line, flipping wildly in an effort to escape. Then, just as suddenly, the fish flipped loose from the line and dropped back into the hole in the ice and disappeared.

"Oh, rats!" The fisherman turned around angrily and said, "Now look what happened! Couldn't you wait?"

"Are you Johnny Argyle?" Mario Garcia said.

The young man stood up. Donna and Abbey recognized him as the blond boy Rick Roberts had been yelling at just before the curtain closed on the fateful day of the last "Teenage Talent Show."

"Yes, I am." The blue eyes shifted uneasily to each one of them, then back to Mario. "What do you want? Is something wrong?"

"It all depends," Mario said. "The police want you for questioning — in connection with the death of Rick Roberts."

Johnny Argyle made a small sound from the back of his throat. His eyes rolled upward, and he fainted dead away on the ground.

Though his blackout lasted no more than a few minutes, when Johnny Argyle came to and saw the faces of Donna Rockford and Detective Garcia above him, he still seemed in a different world.

"Where am I?" he said.

"You're all right, Johnny," Mario assured him. "Just take it easy a little while longer. Don't try to get up."

They helped him to his feet, led him to

a stunted log beside the frozen pond, and sat him down. Abbey spread her muffler on the ice-covered log, and Donna reached into her backpack, poured a cup of steaming coffee, and brought it to Johnny's lips.

After a few sips, he regained his color. "I don't understand it," Johnny said. "I never fainted before in my life. You did say Rick Roberts is — is *dead*?"

"That's right." Mario resumed his official manner. "What do you know about it?"

"Nothing," Johnny said quickly. "I — I can't believe it! What happened? An auto accident? A h-heart attack?"

"Nothing like that," Mario said. "We've been trying all week to locate you, Johnny."

"Me? Why?" Johnny said, frightened.

"Well, what were you doing in the studio that day? You were supposed to have left on vacation."

"I — I just came back to the studio to talk to — to say good-bye to Bonnie," Johnny said. "Honestly, that's all."

"But the show was about to start in a few minutes. What time could you possibly have spent with her?" Mario Garcia, all policeman now, was zeroing in.

Donna's heart stopped as Johnny, his face fearful, said, "We — we had a fight the night before. I wanted to say good-bye to her and to Mr. Reilly, that's all."

"Did you go up to talk to Mr. Reilly? Think carefully," Mario said, his eyes never leaving the boy's face.

"I — I don't get it," Johnny said. "All right, I did go up to the catwalk to see Mr. Reilly. What about it?"

Detective Garcia said, slowly and menacingly, "Was that before or after the parallel bars dropped on Rick Roberts and killed him?"

"What?!" Johnny Argyle's hand flew to his throat. Then his eyes narrowed. "You think I had something to do with that? Or Mr. Reilly?" He clapped a hand over his mouth.

"I think I should warn you that anything you say may be held in evidence against you," Mario Garcia said, removing a folded paper from inside his jacket.

Johnny looked around fearfully. "Don't worry, I'm not saying another word. You can't make me."

Mario stepped forward and held out the paper. As Donna and Abbey watched, he said solemnly, "John Argyle, I'm taking you back to Philadelphia with me, where you will be arraigned on suspicion of murder. This is a warrant for your arrest."

SIXTEEN

Thursday, 5:00 P.M.: Eight days to the hour since Rick Roberts had died.

In police headquarters, where Detective Garcia was delivering Johnny Argyle in custody to Captain Gavin, Donna waited for the proper moment. While two uniformed policeman stood near Johnny, one on either side, both Donna and Abbey were upset to see how the young boy had grown increasingly sad since they'd left Minnesota by plane five hours earlier.

"I feel terrible for him," Abbey said. "I think Mario is a stinker for arresting him."

"He had no choice," Donna said. "Look at the way Johnny clammed up. As if he's got a lot of information he isn't giving."

"Do you think he *is* keeping secrets?" Abbey asked anxiously.

"I do," Donna said.

"But if they book him for murder, won't that be a blot on his record for the rest of his life?" Abbey asked. "Suppose he's innocent?"

Donna stood there, her eyes far away, as if she were staring into a distant land. Her lips moved, and she was saying something to herself that sounded like, " . . . but why would he? . . . He won't talk. . . . No sense. . . . No sense at all. Unless —" Donna's eyes lit up. "Of course!" she said aloud. "How stupid I've been!" She looked over at Mario Garcia, who was standing before the wooden railing separating Johnny Argyle and himself from Captain Gavin behind the desk.

"No! Don't do it, Mario!" Donna said.

Detective Garcia turned. "What are you talking about, Donna? Don't do what?"

Donna was by his side in an instant. "Captain Gavin! Don't book him, please!"

Captain Gavin, gray-haired, gray-eyed, and somber, looked up from his records.

"Do you know what you're saying, Donna? This is an arraignment for murder, and you're telling us to lay off?"

"Captain Gavin! Mario! Please don't do this yet. I'm asking you to get all the suspects in this case together." Donna's hazel eyes willed both men to listen. Johnny Argyle, with a uniformed policeman on either side of him, cast his eyes about like a trapped animal looking for some means of escape.

"This is most unusual," Captain Gavin said. "We've already sworn out a warrant for his arrest, as you know." He looked briefly at Donna. "I'll admit that was very smart deducing on your part that led to the defendant's whereabouts. We'd have had quite a delay without it. But what you're asking now, Donna, is more than I'm prepared to do."

"Get everybody down to Studio 13 — now!" Donna implored the police captain. "I promise you won't be sorry, Captain."

"How can you make a statement like that?" Captain Gavin's hawk eyes bored into Donna's face.

"Get them all together, Captain, please." Donna took a deep breath. "I'll admit that all through this case, there's been nothing to grab hold of. But we don't have to whistle in the dark anymore, Captain." She paused again for breath. *"I know who killed Rick Roberts!"*

Thursday, 9:00 P.M. — at Studio 13.

They were all present — on command from Captain John Gavin of Police Precinct 88. The invited guests were seated on folding chairs onstage, right of center. Everyone, except Mr. Reilly, was there who had in any way been significantly involved in what was now known as "The Last Show."

Up front sat Abe Hazelkorn, producer;

beside him, the beautiful blond actress, Lana Lawrence; next to them, Rex Vicente, orchestra leader; then, behind them, David Gould, audio man; Bonnie Reilly, pale and looking extremely frightened; Monte Clark, distinguished white-haired announcer, looking nervous; Johnny Argyle, jittery teenager, seated between Mario Garcia and a uniformed policeman, frequently glancing over at Bonnie Reilly, who somehow managed to avoid Johnny's eyes; Mrs. Argyle, chic in a trim black suit, made of a worn but stylish twill fabric of very good quality; a middle-aged man with brown hair, brown eyes, brown suit, perched alertly on the edge of his chair — Charles Grey, assistant to Howard Reilly. In the front row, at the extreme end, Donna Rockford, looking alert and misleadingly wide awake in a navy-blue-and-white sports top and faded jeans; her sister Abbey, sleepy-eyed but gorgeous in an apricot velour sweatshirt and jeans.

In the auditorium, a few people were sitting in the third and fourth rows, but it was too dark to see who they were from the stage.

Captain Gavin called everyone to order. "I want to thank you all for coming here at this hour. I promise you that you will not be kept here unnecessarily. And now let me turn this meeting over to Detective Mario Garcia. Mario?"

Detective Garcia, in a rumpled brown suit that might well have been the one in which he had made an airplane trip halfway across the continent, stood up and walked to the front of the onstage group.

"Unfortunately, the one man who could possibly clear up the mystery of Rick Roberts' death — Howard Reilly — is unable to give information at this point, although" — he smiled at Bonnie — "he is pretty definitely making a recovery from his illness." He took a deep breath. "We could wait a few days, when Mr. Reilly will be sufficiently recuperated to confirm or deny what happens here today. The reason we do not wish to wait any longer is that each of you, as you doubtless know, has been under suspicion of one sort or another in connection with the Roberts case."

"You can say that again," Abe Hazelkorn said. "My staff has been unable to function. I appreciate this inquiry, no matter what it brings."

Lana Lawrence looked at Abe Hazelkorn, as if trying to stop him, but he shook his head. "No use, Lana. Let's get it all out in the open."

"Let's get on with it, Detective Garcia," Captain Gavin said. "They know why they're here."

"In that case, I'll yield the floor to Donna Rockford," Mario said, stepping back and retreating to his chair beside Johnny Argyle.

Donna walked to where Mario had stood. She held a small group of white file cards that she glanced at as if to refresh her memory. Then she put them down and started to speak.

She began with Abe Hazelkorn. "The first break in this case began in your apartment, Mr. Hazelkorn, on Sunday, when you made that delicious brunch for my sister and me." He looked at her warily but said nothing. "You explained that the fish was spotted-brown trout — and said it came from near the Canadian border, right next to Minnesota. You also mentioned *how* this fish was caught. It needed a special lure, you said."

"Why are you looking at me?" Johnny Argyle said, defensively. "Sure I was fishing for brown-spotted trout, and sure I was using a Pink Candy number two plastic worm, but that was a coincidence."

"Not exactly," Abe Hazelkorn said. "Remember when you mentioned that fish to me, Johnny? About a month ago, I believe." Johnny nodded uncertainly. "I frequently have exceptional fish flown in — from various places. So I got in touch with a fishery in Saskatchewan and they expressed one to me." He smiled at Abbey. "Pretty good, wasn't it?"

"Good? It was sensational!" Abbey would have continued, but Donna cut in.

"I phoned *Field & Stream* magazine and checked the fish and the lure, and they mentioned Voyageur State Park in Minnesota," Donna said. "Suddenly it all added up. Johnny was taking his first vacation on his own — so he chose a fishing vacation near where his dad had always gone." She looked at Johnny Argyle, who flushed and nodded his head.

"To continue," Donna turned to the glamorous movie star beside Mr. Hazelkorn. "Miss Lawrence, you had plenty of reason to hate Rick Roberts — if we can believe the newspapers."

Lana Lawrence's voice was low and carefully modulated. "It's true, Miss Rockford. Rick pretty nearly wrecked my career for good." She instantly added, "But I wouldn't ever, *ever* have tried to hurt him in any way. Not in any way."

"You disappeared so quickly after the accident, leaving no word," Donna said. "Didn't you realize how that would look?"

"I didn't know there was any possibility of — of *murder*," Lana said, her huge, golden brown eyes wide.

Mario Garcia spoke up. "It was obvious to us that anyone who wanted Rick Roberts out of the way could easily have arranged for Howard Reilly to place the parallel bars on the wrong flies overhead. Including," he added grimly, "Reilly himself. He had plenty of reason to hate Roberts."

"Everyone here had a possible motive," Donna said. "We're here tonight to pin the responsibility for Rick Roberts' death on the person who caused it. If you'll let me go on, I think we'll have the answer."

"Go ahead, Miss Rockford," the white-haired Monte Clark said. "We're listening."

Donna said, "We've covered Miss Lawrence and Howard Reilly, two people who had every reason to hate Rick Roberts. Let's go quickly to these two men." She indicated David Gould, plumply spilling over the edge of his chair, then looked at Rex Vicente beside him. "Mr. Gould, your reason for disliking Rick Roberts isn't apparent to me. But I did see something that you did at the cemetery. . . ."

"I can explain," the chubby man with the beard said, frowning. "Can't I, Abe?"

"Go right ahead, Dave," the producer said.

"You're very observant," Mr. Gould said to Donna. "You saw me take this." He reached into his jacket and pulled out a black, plastic-covered object. He took it out of the wrapping to reveal a cassette. "I made this only two minutes before 'The Teenage Talent Show' began last Tuesday." He looked keenly at Donna. "Want to hear what I recorded?"

"I sure would," Mario Garcia said. "We picked up a shot of you passing it to Hazelkorn at the funeral." He looked knowingly at Donna, who was thinking, *Why didn't you tell me, Mario? Were you afraid I'd get the jump on you?*

"All right, here it comes." David Gould turned the cassette recorder up in volume. There was a hushed silence as they heard the voice of Rick Roberts:

"*Out!* I want Howard Reilly out! Isn't that what I told you, Abe?" Rick Roberts was speaking.

"Rick," Abe Hazelkorn's voice said, "have a heart. Howard's been with this studio for over twenty years. . . ."

"Don't give me that sob story about how great he used to be. I can't get this show on week after week with memories — I need top people."

"The union won't allow it. . . ."

"I don't care about the union. I'll dream up a story you can hand them."

"But you can't do that. . . ."

"But me no buts. He *goes*."

"You can turn that off now," Detective Garcia said. "We get the gist."

"Why did you record that?" Donna asked Mr. Gould.

"Reilly was getting a raw deal. If he was dropped from the show at that time, his benefits would have been a third of what he was entitled to. Poor Reilly had twenty-three years at WGBL. He'd earned every cent of a full pension," Gould said. "I recorded evidence so Reilly could appeal his case when he got fired."

"I have to apologize to you, Mr. Gould," Donna said. She reached in a pocket and took out a brass button. "When my sister and I were attacked a few days ago, I managed to grab this." She grinned shamefacedly.

"There was one missing from your jacket when we visited you a couple of days ago."

"Correction," Mr. Gould said. "There were two missing."

"That was just life in Philadelphia," Detective Garcia said. "A couple of muggers in ski masks. They were picked up yesterday."

"How about letting me have that button?" David Gould said. "I'm a bachelor and I live alone and I'll never buy another one."

Donna handed it to him, smiling. "It's all yours." Her face grew serious. "So now you all know as much as I know about Mr. Hazelkorn, Miss Lawrence, Mr. Gould. . . ." She hesitated. "That brings us to you, Mr. Vicente. There's one little item you can clear up for us, if you will."

"Sure, anything." His Adam's apple bobbed above the ascot tie. "I mean, if I can."

"Last week, when we unexpectedly showed up at Studio 13, you were ramming some papers into your pocket." Donna's eyes met his. "Want to tell us what they were?"

"Sure, I've got them right here." The orchestra leader took some pages out of his coat pocket. "I wrote this for — for Rick."

"What is it?" Detective Garcia asked.

"Well, I know I probably got on Rick's nerves, sometimes." He gulped. "And I hated the way he was always ribbing me. But I'm sorry Rick is dead." He showed the ruled music sheets to the detective. "It's a requiem I wrote in his memory."

Monte Clark, the announcer, spoke up for the first time. "That's very decent, Rex. Very decent." He paused. "He was very rough on you, Rex. As he was with all of us at one time or another."

Rex Vicente flushed with pleasure. "Thank you," he said. "But he was a talented man, and he was young, and it's a pity he had to die."

"Mr. Clark," Donna said, "did you have any special reason to resent Rick? Did he interfere with your career, or your personal life?"

The announcer straightened his shoulders. "Certainly not. He was never my friend — but then Rick was close to no one. I stayed away from his funeral because" — he gave a self-conscious little laugh — "because I can't stand them. Funerals — I mean. Grisly affairs. Uncivilized."

There was a moment's uncomfortable silence after that statement; then Donna spoke up. "Now we come to the two remaining people" — she glanced at Bonnie Reilly, then at Johnny Argyle behind her — "who had the opportunity, if not the motive, to kill Rick Roberts."

Bonnie Reilly slunk lower in her chair and looked at the floor. Johnny Argyle said, "Now, look here, you can't say that about Bonnie or me." His face reddened. "Mr. Roberts was like an angel from heaven to my family. Because of him, my mother's life was probably saved. And I got a job, and — oh, what's the use!"

He bit his lip and added, "If you think I killed him, you're wrong. He gave me a note to bring to Howard Reilly."

"He did?" Donna said. "Want to tell us about it?"

"All right," Johnny said. "Here's what happened. He wanted me to take a note up to Howard Reilly, telling him to change the position of the parallel bars up on the flies. I told him not to do it."

"Why?" Mario Garcia asked skeptically.

"I — I told him it was too late to make a change like that." Johnny gulped, then cleared his throat.

"What made you say that?" Mario demanded.

"I didn't think Mr. Reilly could make the change that fast," Johnny said, in his unconvincing manner.

"Then what happened?" Mario asked.

"He yelled at me. Then he grabbed the instruction sheet from me and said he'd bring it up himself and I should change the blue marker on the stage."

"And did you?" Donna asked gently.

"I had to," Johnny said. "I moved the marker to where he said he wanted it."

"Then what did you do?"

"I left." Johnny shrugged his shoulders. "I did what I was supposed to and I left. I had a plane to make."

Mario took a deep breath. "Rick Roberts was killed because the parallel bars fell on him. Admit it, fella — you didn't bother to move the tape on the floor — so the bars came right down on Roberts!"

"No! No!" Johnny covered his face in his hands and moaned. "No! It wasn't like that!"

"Like what?" Mario said instantly.

Johnny took his hands away from his face and saw Mario staring at him. "What are you trying to say? That I didn't move the tape? But I did!"

"All we have is your word for what happened in this studio that day," Mario said. "Don't forget, we can check out your story with Howard Reilly."

Johnny Argyle started to cry. "I didn't kill him! I swear I didn't kill Rick Roberts!"

Bonnie Reilly shot up from her seat and went over to him. She put her hands on his head and said, "Don't cry, Johnny. Don't cry. I know you didn't do it. I *know* you're not lying."

Mario Garcia turned on the young girl. "You *know*? How can you be so sure, Bonnie — unless you know who *did* arrange that convenient accident?"

Bonnie stared at the detective wildly. She said, "What are you saying? Are you trying to say that I — I . . ." She couldn't finish.

"I'm not saying that," Mario Garcia said. "It could have been any one of you three — Johnny, or you" — he paused — "or — your father."

"No, no! He didn't do it! My father is innocent!" She slammed her fist against her chest. "I confess! I did it! Johnny didn't do it. My father didn't do it. I did!"

Donna came up beside her and said, "Tell us how, Bonnie. How did you do it?"

"I — I ran up to the rafters and went along the catwalk and waited till my father had his back turned and I moved the parallel bars right to where they would fall on Rick! I did it!"

Her fists clenched, she stood her ground, looking defiantly around at the others.

"It's no use, Bonnie." Donna came over to the girl, put her arm around her, and led her to a seat. "Sit down, please. I know what you did."

Bonnie looked up in fright and stifled a sob with the back of her hand. "Oh, no! You can't know — you can't!"

"I know more than you think, Bonnie. It took a while to figure out who was making those attacks on my sister and me. And then to figure out why." Donna paused. "But first, I'm going to ask a favor of Detective Garcia."

When Mario got up and came over to her, Donna whispered something urgently to him, and he walked hurriedly away to a wall phone in the backstage corridor. Donna then went back to her position beside Bonnie.

"Where were we? Oh, yes — yes, Bonnie. You thought that either Johnny or your father killed Rick Roberts — through carelessness or deliberately, right?" As Bonnie sat with her lips tight together, Donna went on. "Answer me, please! Isn't that what you thought? Isn't that why you tried to stop me from investigating? Why you sent those anonymous notes — slashed the tires of my car — attacked my sister in the alley behind the dorm?"

Very slowly, Bonnie raised her tear-stained face. "Don't . . . please don't," she whispered. "I confess — everything." Her face was ravaged.

At that moment, Mario Garcia came back to the group, his forefinger and thumb ringed in an "A-okay" gesture.

"You were right, Donna. I got Reilly's doctor and he let me talk to his patient and say what you suggested I should ask him." Mario heaved a deep sigh. "It's true. It happened the way you thought."

"What's going on here?" Captain Gavin demanded. "I want to know everything — now."

Detective Garcia said, "This is Donna Rockford's ballgame, Captain. She has the answers — let her tell it. Okay?"

The police captain grunted and sat down. "All right. Let's hear it, Donna."

Donna said, "Thank you," and turned back to Bonnie. "You did all that to try to protect Johnny or your father, Bonnie. But they didn't have anything to do with Rick Roberts' death. You did all of that for nothing!"

Captain Gavin interrupted. "You're saying that we still don't know why Rick Roberts was killed?"

"No, Captain Gavin," Donna said quietly. "I

do know who arranged for Rick Roberts to die."

"Then who?" the captain said grimly. "Who did it? *Who?*"

Donna answered slowly, each word clear, incisive: *"Rick Roberts was the cause of his own death!"*

The small group of people heard the announcement and reacted with deep shock.

"Can you prove that?" Captain Gavin demanded.

"She can, Captain," Mario Garcia said. "Go on, Donna.

"Rick Roberts was killed by his own vanity." Instantly David Gould and Abe Hazelkorn exchanged knowing glances.

"He did give a last-minute order to move the equipment," Donna said. "Thanks to my sister Abbey and her fan magazines, I got a clue to the reason." She turned to the glamorous Miss Lawrence. "I saw you come to the studio. You sat down front on the right aisle. From where you were sitting, if Rick Roberts stood onstage as planned, he would have been standing with his *left* profile facing you. But that wouldn't do for Mr. Roberts. It was his bad profile. In his vanity, he wanted you to see him at his best, even though your relationship had ended long before."

"Of course," David Gould said somberly. "That's the way it had to be." He added, "And someone *had* moved the tape. I'll testify to that."

"Donna told me to ask Howard Reilly if Rick Roberts told him to move the parallel bars, and if Howard Reilly refused, and then, if Rick moved the bars himself," Mario explained to Captain Gavin. "That's what happened. Reilly *knew* it wasn't safe — but couldn't stop Rick. When the rope holding the bars in the new position broke away, the shock is what brought on Reilly's stroke."

"I can't believe it," Lana Lawrence said. "I came to the show that day to be with Abe. And to warn Rick that he'd better not try to spoil things between Abe and me."

"Lana and I are engaged to be married," Abe Hazelkorn said. He turned to Lana. "Nothing he could have said or done would have changed my feelings for you."

It was Abe Hazelkorn who summed it all up neatly.

"After all the people he treated so miserably," Mr. Hazelkorn said, "the poor guy turned out to be his own worst enemy."

It was the next morning. Abbey was proudly waving the morning newspaper at the group gathered around the dining table in the Rockford home. The headlines read:

YOUNG GIRL SLEUTH HELPS SOLVE MYSTERY OF STUDIO 13!

"Look, folks — they're finally giving credit to my sister!" Abbey boasted.

Around the table were seated Dr. Rockford and Mr. Rockford, Mario Garcia, Abbey's friend Jane, Donna, and Abbey.

"You've got to tell us," Mario said, helping himself to a second portion of bacon and eggs. "How did you know it was Bonnie who was trying to stop you?"

"She left clues all over, poor thing," Donna said. "She lied about not having been out in the snow. She's as Irish as a shamrock — she even bought an 'Erin go bragh' stamp for that mysterious letter. It means 'Ireland goes free' and — oh, it was obvious — she didn't want anyone to investigate the case."

Mario said, "She's being put on probation for one year for pulling all those stunts." He looked at Donna. "I think you'll be interested in a statement Rick Roberts' mother gave us."

"Donna! How did you know that Diana Strober was Rick Roberts' mother?" Abbey said.

"That was easy," Donna said. "The poor lady's room was full of puzzle books. Crosswords and anagrams. Think about it, Abbey. 'Strober' is an anagram — a rearrangement of the same letters — for what?"

"Roberts! Strober! That's right!" Abbey said ecstatically.

"That isn't all," Mario said. "Mrs. Strober's boss, the one in charge of the nursing home, told us that Mrs. Strober — I mean Mrs. Roberts — was in New England visiting a lawyer. Her husband left a sizable insurance policy that Rick Roberts had taken the money from the year before. Now that the money is hers, Mrs. Roberts is putting it into making that nursing home a lot better-looking, buying a few new TV sets, and furniture — things like that."

"Oh, Donna, isn't that great?" Abbey beamed at her sister.

"Our problem," Mr. Rockford said to his wife, "is that we had ourselves two bright young daughters — sometimes *too* bright for their own safety."

Dr. Rockford said, "It isn't easy, is it?" But both parents looked proudly at their children.

At that moment the doorbell rang.

"I'll get it," Donna said. *Oh, I hope it is, I really hope it is,* she thought as she hurried to the door.

She opened it to see — Pete O'Brien. In his arms he held a massive bunch of flowers.

"I just wanted you to have these, Donna." He handed the flowers to her. "It's my way of saying — I've been a dope."

Donna's eyes gleamed. "Oh, Pete," she said, but then broke off as another figure hurried up the walk. It looked familiar to her — it was familiar. It was Matthew Rosen, the police doctor's son.

"Hi, Donna," he said. "Is Abbey home? . . ."

Donna felt herself gently elbowed aside by her sister, who thrust out a welcoming hand. "Oh, Matthew! I'm *so* glad you could make it. Come in! Come in!"

By this time, Detective Mario Garcia was in the front hallway with them. He looked from Donna to Pete, and from Abbey to Matthew.

"Oh, Mario. Don't think I forgot you," Abbey said. "I did think of inviting Lana Lawrence for you, but she *is* getting married. So then I . . ."

Mario put his hat on, buckled his trenchcoat, and said, "Hush your mouth, child. I have piles of reports to make on the Roberts case, so I have to leave now." He stopped and looked squarely at Donna, standing beside Pete. "But I'll be back. . . . Did you hear, Pete? I'll be back."